Mollie couldn't understand it. Just when she had told herself for the tenth time that she would forget about Paul and enjoy the attentions of the other boys, she would catch him looking her way with an expression of such wistful eagerness that her hopes would rise once more. But each time the players took a break, and the other boys crowded around Mollie, Paul continued to hang back.

Mollie didn't know what to do. "Forget about him," she told herself, trying to listen to Raoul's latest story, or Antoine's newest joke.

But when the boys returned to their practice, Mollie couldn't help picking out Paul's tall form as he moved swiftly over the ice, or help noticing his automatic sportsmanship when another player fell, and Paul was the first to help him to his feet.

What was a girl to do?

FAWCETT GIRLS ONLY BOOKS

SISTERS

THREE'S A CROWD #1

TOO LATE FOR LOVE #2

THE KISS #3

SECRETS AT SEVENTEEN #4

ALWAYS A PAIR #5

ON THIN ICE #6

STAR QUALITY #7

MAKING WAVES #8

TOO MANY COOKS #9

OUT OF THE WOODS #10

NEVER A DULL MOMENT #11

MOLLIE IN LOVE #12

SISTERS

MOLLIE IN LOVE

Jennifer Cole

FAWCETT GIRLS ONLY • NEW YORK

RLI:
VL: Grades 5 + up

IL: Grades 6 + up

A Fawcett Girls Only Book
Published by Ballantine Books
Copyright © 1987 by Cloverdale Press, Inc.

All rights reserved under International and Pan-American Copyright Conventions. Published in the United States by Ballantine Books, a division of Random House, Inc., New York, and simultaneously in Canada by Random House of Canada Limited, Toronto.

Library of Congress Catalog Card Number: 86-91831

ISBN 0-449-13212-9

All the characters in this book are fictitious and any resemblance to actual persons, living or dead, is purely coincidental.

Manufactured in the United States of America

First Edition: June 1987

The author wishes to express special thanks to
Louise Paquet
Margaret Zavitz
Carol Thomas
and, in particular,
Johanne Carrier, of the
Delegation du Quebec,
for their generous assistance and
true Canadian bonhomie.

Chapter 1

"*N*icole, come quick! I think you're in trouble," fourteen-year-old Mollie Lewis shouted between breaths. She was panting from her frantic dash from the telephone to the back porch.

Nicole Lewis, at seventeen the eldest of the three Lewis sisters, had been sitting on the patio glancing through a packet of photographs. She jumped up, letting the snapshots fall to the ground.

"*Qu'est-ce que c'est?* Is it Mother?" Nicole could think of nothing she'd done wrong lately. Of course, she *had* stayed out with a group of friends until dawn on graduation night, but her parents had given their permission. How many times did a girl graduate from high school, for goodness' sake? Anyway, that was already over a week ago.

"No," Mollie answered, ignoring Nicole's French expression; the whole Lewis family was accustomed to her passion for all things French. "It's

Madame Preston, the French teacher. She's so upset, she can hardly talk. She was spouting French at me so fast I couldn't understand a word!"

Cindy Lewis, sixteen, who had been occupying the other chaise lounge as she read the latest postcard from her boyfriend Grant, frowned at her younger sister. "How can Nicole be in trouble with Madame Preston? School's been out for over a week. Use your head for once, airbrain!"

"Well, she's very agitated about something," Mollie argued in her own defense, tossing her blond curls. "You'd better hurry, Nicole."

But Nicole had already disappeared through the French doors, rushing toward the telephone.

Cindy, looking slightly downcast, turned her attention back to the short message on the postcard: "Surf's great; wish you were here. Love, Grant."

Turning over the card, she surveyed the full-color photograph of Waikiki Beach, noting several bikini-clad girls ornamenting the white sand. Terrific. Her boyfriend was in Hawaii visiting his grandparents, having a wonderful time, and probably every girl on the beach had her eye on his handsome face and tanned, muscular body. Just great.

Cindy frowned and ran one hand through her short, sun-streaked blond hair. Not one to spend time worrying about her appearance, Cindy knew that her trim, athletic body and golden tan would compare favorably to those of the girls on the postcard. But she was here, and Grant was there!

She chewed on her lip. There was plenty of good surfing on the nearby Santa Barbara beaches, but it just wasn't the same without Grant here. And she knew about those famous Hawaiian waves. She was dying to try surfing there.

Grant had already sent two cheerful, if brief, postcards, so she knew he hadn't forgotten her, but still ...

"Cheer up, Cindy," Mollie said from beside her. "Grant'll only be gone two months."

"Two months! That's an eternity," Cindy groaned. "Has the paper come?"

"It's on the hall table."

Cindy stood up and slid open the doors that led inside the red-roofed, Spanish-style house that was home to the Lewis clan.

"Still checking for bargain flights to Hawaii?" Mollie asked. "You know Mom and Dad will never let you go; you've been arguing with them all week."

"I don't see why not," Cindy grumbled.

"I don't either; I'd love to go somewhere this summer," Mollie said with a sigh. "New York, Mexico, the Caribbean—I'm not choosy. But you know what Mom said about you being too young—"

Cindy made a face and disappeared inside the house.

Left alone on the sunny patio, Mollie picked up the snapshots Nicole had dropped in her rush to the phone. They had been taken the night of her graduation. Mollie studied the pictures—slim, graceful, brown-haired Nicole and short, plump Bitsy, clinging together, teary-eyed, as the two friends realized that high school was really behind them forever; Nicole, blue eyes glowing, looked luminous with excitement in her white gown and mortarboard as she made her speech in front of the whole auditorium.

Mollie felt a surge of pride; not everybody's sister graduated as valedictorian! Nicole was really something—beautiful, and smart, too. Sometimes Mollie felt awfully inadequate by comparison. It was true that Nicole insisted that Mollie's well-developed figure was pleasing, and that her big blue eyes and cheerful smile were as attractive as any girl could wish. But Mollie still thought she'd rather be tall and slim, like her sister.

She sighed. All her life she was going to feel like an also-ran, she thought darkly, curling her petite frame up on the comfortable chaise lounge. That was the worst thing about being the youngest of three.

This discouraging thought was interrupted by Nicole's return. Mollie, remembering the mysterious phone call, looked up, eager to find out what it was about.

"Tell me," she demanded, staring at her older sister, who seemed a bit dazed. "Did you flunk your exam and end up not really being valedictorian, after all? Are they going to take away your award?"

Nicole, who had never flunked a test in her life, didn't seem to hear. She was lost in her own private dream. Graduation had been both joyous and sad, as she realized that one part of her life had ended. But college was coming up quickly;

she had lots to do as she prepared, for the first time in her life, to leave home. Nicole could hardly sleep at night, just thinking of the exciting new experiences that lay ahead of her. She wasn't a child any longer—anything could happen. She was on the brink of adulthood, just beginning a whole new existence. The idea was staggering.

And it all was beginning even sooner than she had expected!

"Nicole!" her irrepressible younger sister demanded. "Talk to me!"

Nicole answered slowly, still lost in her thoughts. "That was Madame Preston, from school."

"I *know* that," Mollie said, squirming in her seat with impatience. "Why was she so upset?"

"She wasn't upset; she was excited. She nominated me for a special honors course in French. She said she didn't tell me earlier because she didn't want me to be disappointed if I wasn't chosen. But I've been selected!"

Mollie's air of anticipation quickly faded. "Is that all? Another class? Who wants to spend the summer studying? Do you really intend to do it, Nicole? You've got some modeling jobs already scheduled."

"I'll tell the agency I can't take any more after this week." Nicole, who had already decided that modeling wasn't the most satisfying part of her life, sounded indifferent. "I've got to check on plane fares."

"Plane fares—what are you talking about?" Mollie looked up in surprise. "Isn't this class at the UCSB in town?"

"No," Nicole answered, her tone blissful. "It's in Quebec." With that she disappeared through the French doors, leaving a stunned Mollie behind.

"*Quebec?*" Mollie looked outraged. "That's in Canada! That's a foreign country; this isn't *fair!*"

Chapter 2

*W*hen *Laura Lewis returned home late that* afternoon after a busy day at her catering business, Movable Feasts, Nicole was waiting with her big news.

"Quebec? An honors class in French? Nicole, what a marvelous opportunity," Mrs. Lewis said, setting down her briefcase. "I'm so proud of you."

"And I'll get to stay in the college dorm; it'll be almost like a trial run for this fall," Nicole told her mother. "And in Quebec—the only French-speaking area in North America. *Mon dieu.* Isn't this wonderful?"

"It isn't fair," Mollie murmured to herself, taking a vicious swipe at a head of lettuce. The whole family was aware of Nicole's predilection for all things French, but still, why did Nicole always have all the luck?

Nicole hugged her mother, the whole story spilling out in an enthusiastic if incoherent rush. Winston, the Lewises' big Newfoundland, sniffed hopefully at the strips of steak forgotten on the cutting board.

"Winston, don't you dare. That's for my beef Stroganoff!" Nicole turned just in time. The big black dog looked absurdly guilty, and, tail down, padded back to his blanket.

Mollie went back to her half-made salad, but her expression was bleak. Why did all the exciting things happen to Nicole: valedictorian of her high school class, part-time model, sought after by tons of boys. Mollie felt increasingly forlorn. And now a terrific vacation trip to an exciting province that Mollie had never seen, leaving her little sister to die of boredom at home. Mollie sniffed.

"Don't put in so much onion, Mollie," Nicole commanded heartlessly. Mollie, who was cutting carrots, not onions, threw her sister a dirty look.

At the dinner table that night, Mr. Lewis listened to Nicole's news and also seemed impressed.

"That's wonderful, Nicole. Although I hate to see you leave home even earlier than we'd planned," he said.

Nicole, who was serving the chocolate mousse she had made to celebrate, paused to give her father a hug. "It's only for four weeks, Dad. I'll be back home before I leave for the East Coast and college in September."

Mollie stuck a spoon into her creamy mousse and sighed. Cindy was more vocal in her complaint.

"You're letting Nicole waltz off to Canada, and

you won't let me go to Hawaii, which is part of our own country, in case you've forgotten!" The middle Lewis, her green eyes bright with anger, stormed at her parents.

"I don't need a geography lesson, Cindy," Mrs. Lewis said, sighing. "We've been through this already."

"I don't see why I can't—"

"Cindy, you're too young to spend several weeks alone so far from home."

"Grant—"

"Grant is staying with relatives."

"I could—"

Laura Lewis's tone sharpened. "No, you couldn't. His grandparents have a small apartment. Grant told us that before he left; he's sleeping on the living-room couch. They have no room for visitors. Besides, well-mannered people do not invite themselves to other people's homes!"

Richard Lewis looked over his glasses at his rebellious middle daughter. "That'll do, young lady."

Cindy, her expression still stormy, nevertheless knew when it was time to shut up. But she sat and seethed inwardly, and as soon as possible, stalked away from the table in a sulky silence.

Nicole, watching her sister go, felt a momentary pang. She knew how discontented Cindy felt, and she wished things were different. But still, she refused to let her sister—make that sisters, Nicole thought, glancing over at Mollie's glum expression—dim her excitement. They would have their chance someday. This was Nicole's moment, and how glorious it was!

Nicole hurried through her part of the chores so she could get back to her bedroom and finish filling out all the necessary forms for the course. Because Madame Preston, who had suffered a bad case of flu in the spring, had been late submitting Nicole's name, time was very short, and Nicole didn't want to risk her wonderful chance by missing the deadline.

She sent her forms off by special delivery, and for the next few days anxiously awaited the postman every morning for confirmation and details about the course.

Cindy, watching her sister linger by the kitchen window, couldn't quite subdue her feelings of envy. "Don't worry. Nothing ever goes wrong for *you.*"

Nicole looked around, her expression genuinely sympathetic. "Cindy, I'm really sorry you can't go to Hawaii."

Cindy, prepared for a brisk exchange of words, was unnerved by this gentle rejoinder.

"It's not your fault," she muttered. "But it's going to be worse than ever with you gone. Bad enough that you'll be leaving in the fall."

Nicole, startled to see that her usually unsentimental sister was sincere, gave her a quick hug. With all their differences, the Lewis sisters had always been close. "I'll miss you, too," she said.

"I don't know about that. You'll be busy with class work, new friends; you won't have much time to think about us," Cindy told her. "It'll seem pretty strange not having you around."

"Not to mention that you'll have more chores to do," Nicole said with a grin.

Cindy laughed reluctantly. A thump from outside the house made them both jump.

"There's the mail!" Nicole cried, running for the door. Cindy followed close behind her.

"Bills, junk mail—how can we get so many circulars?" Nicole muttered to herself. Then she held up a long envelope triumphantly. "It's here!"

"Open it," Cindy urged, catching some of her older sister's excitement. "What do they say?"

Nicole dropped the rest of the mail onto the hall table and ripped open the envelope. She scanned the first letter. "All my applications are in order."

"Naturally," Cindy said, pushing away her feelings of envy, trying not to let the green-eyed monster overwhelm her again. "Well, I'm really glad for you, Nicole." She turned toward the kitchen to bury her sorrows in a dish of chocolate-chip ice cream. When she was just about to dig in, she heard Nicole let out a sob and she ran back to the hall to join her sister.

"What's wrong?"

Nicole had both hands to her face and she looked about ready to cry.

"The dorm is full! They don't have room for me," she moaned.

Chapter 3

Cindy, who hadn't really meant to jinx Nicole's chance for a terrific summer trip, felt guilty anyhow.

"It's because I was so late getting the forms in," Nicole moaned for the tenth time. "If I'd been earlier, I would have gotten a reservation before all the dorm rooms were taken."

"Can't they squeeze you in somewhere—a broom closet, maybe?" Mollie inquired, trying to be helpful.

"She's not Cinderella, shrimp," Cindy retorted. Nicole was too depressed to answer.

Mrs. Lewis, listening with a grave face, said more practically, "What did the college suggest, Nicole?"

"They sent a short list of private homes that take boarders, and I've been on the phone all day. There's not one single vacancy left!" Again Nicole looked as if she was on the verge of tears.

Cinders, hearing the despondent tone in her

voice, came to wrap himself around the eldest Lewis sister's ankles. Nicole reached down to pat the mottled gray fur and the young cat purred in response. But Nicole still frowned.

"Mother, what am I going to do? I can't pass up an opportunity like this."

"How about a hotel?" Mollie suggested.

Laura Lewis looked at her oldest daughter and sighed. "We'll check, Nicole, and see what we can find. But Quebec City is a popular place for summer tourists; I'm not sure we'll even find a hotel room available."

Nicole, unable to contain her disappointment any longer, nodded, and picking up the stack of books about Quebec and Canadian history from the library, headed for her room, where she could cry in peace.

Even Cindy looked gloomy, although she couldn't help thinking that no one had seemed overly sympathetic when she was denied permission to go to Hawaii.

"Doesn't seem like any of the Lewis sisters are going to have a good summer," she murmured to Winston. "Except for Mollie; she'll go to the beach and fall in love a few dozen times, as usual."

"I will not," Mollie said indignantly when she overheard Cindy's *sotto voce* remark. "I'm growing up, Cindy, in case you haven't noticed. And anyway, it's been at least two months since I was last in love."

"You're right, I haven't noticed," Cindy hooted. Taking one more brownie from the plate on the kitchen counter, she escaped into the hall while

Mollie looked around for something to throw at her. Cindy saw a banana heading her way, then watched it hit the hall floor with a squish.

"Mollie!" Mrs. Lewis said sharply. "Clean that up this minute!"

"Slave all day," Mollie muttered. "That's all I ever do." She picked up the abused fruit from the carpet and headed for the sanctity of her littered bedroom.

Mrs. Lewis, left alone with Winston, sighed. "Heaven help me," she told the big dog. "It's going to be a long summer."

Richard Lewis, surveying the silent group around the dinner table that night, had to chuckle at the collection of long faces. "Cheer up, girls," he told his daughters. "It can't be that bad."

"Mais oui," Nicole disagreed. "It can be."

"I don't suppose I dare ask about your day," her father said, looking at his eldest daughter over his glasses.

"I've been calling hotels in Quebec City all day," she told him with a frown.

"Aiee," Mr. Lewis groaned, "my phone bill!"

Cindy, despite her sympathy for his sister, remembered her long arguments over Hawaii and couldn't help putting in, "I don't see why Nicole's old enough to stay in a hotel by herself in a strange city, and I'm not!"

"I'm *older* than you are, that's why." Nicole turned on her sister sharply, wounded by this unexpected attack. "And I'm about to leave for college, anyhow."

"Yes, but a dorm isn't quite the same as a hotel," Cindy pointed out. "Anyhow, you're not that much older!"

"Girls." Mr. Lewis called them to order. Looking from one angry face to another, he shook his head. "This is not exactly a picture of family harmony."

Cindy, about to retort, took a look at her father's stern face and thought better of it. But she grimaced at the roast beef on her plate.

"Did you find a room, Nicole?" Mollie asked meekly.

Nicole sighed. "No," she admitted. "Not one hotel had a room available for the whole period."

Mrs. Lewis offered Mollie another slice of beef as she said, "Perhaps it's just as well. I'm afraid Cindy has a point. I'm not thrilled at the thought of you staying alone so long in a hotel."

"Mother!" Nicole sounded outraged. "You don't seem to realize that I'm almost grown up!"

Mrs. Lewis exchanged an ironic glance with her husband. "Indeed, we do," she told her insulted daughter. "But your father and I still have some responsibility for your well being."

Nicole subsided into aggrieved silence. Cindy, her mind filled with pictures of Grant on a white Hawaiian beach, surrounded by girls, shook her head at the offer of more roast beef. Even Mollie, who wasn't dieting this week, turned down another piece of Yorkshire pudding.

Laura Lewis looked around the table. "I think it's just as well that your father and I are getting away this weekend. But I don't want any squabbling while we're gone; I want all three of you in one piece when we get back Sunday."

Cindy, her mind far away, looked up. "Where are you going?"

"You remember," her mother reminded her patiently. "My college reunion in Los Angeles. We'll be gone overnight Saturday for the big get-together."

Mollie sniffed. "I hope you're not going to do anything silly, like dress up in old sixties-style clothes and lovebeads, and put your hair in braids, like Sarah's mother did for her reunion. I mean, how embarrassing!"

Mrs. Lewis grinned. "If I do, I'll be sure that none of your friends see me, Mollie. I won't humiliate you by my senile behavior, I promise."

"I hope not," Mollie said seriously, looking offended when both her parents laughed.

While the girls picked at their dinner, Mr. and Mrs. Lewis discussed the coming weekend. The three sisters, each lost in her own private circle of gloom, ignored frivolous talk about "do you remember?"

The weekend was a disaster. Nicole stayed in her room Saturday, making long-distance calls to Quebec, still without success. Her half-packed bags and the plane ticket on her bureau only increased her depression. Even the cats couldn't cheer her up; Smokey, her elegant gray tail high in the air, stalked out of Nicole's bedroom, miffed at being ignored.

Cindy got up early and went for her usual run,

missing her father's company. They often ran together on weekend mornings but he and Mrs.
Lewis had already left for the drive to Los Angeles. Then she showered, changed, and took her
surfboard down to the beach.

But, although Anna and Duffy welcomed her,
Cindy couldn't forget the great empty space where
Grant should have been.

"Cheer up, Cindy," Anna told her. "Grant'll be
home in August."

"August!" Cindy moaned. "That's an eternity."

She stood up, too despondent to be cheered
by well-meaning efforts, and pulled her board
toward the surf. But even several good waves in a
row didn't cheer her. She returned to the sand in
record time, and Anna raised her brows at her
old friend.

"This *is* serious," she admitted. "If Cindy Lewis
gives up surfing, all is not right with the world!"

"You'd better believe it," Cindy grumbled.

"Have a cookie; I made them myself," Anna
offered.

"No, thanks." Cindy flopped down onto her
beach towel, ignoring Duffy as he rolled his eyes.

"Cindy Lewis turning down food? Nurse, I think
this case is terminal," he quipped.

Cindy didn't even snap at him. Anna looked
concerned. "Come on, Cindy, you can't spend the
summer moping."

"Want to bet?"

A new arrival made them all glance up. It was
Mollie, in her newest bikini.

"What are you doing here, shrimp?"

"Thanks for the welcome," Mollie answered, sitting down gracefully on one end of Cindy's beach towel. "I can't find any of my friends; there are no good-looking guys on the beach—sorry, Duffy," she added, as the redhead pretended to look offended. "And I forgot my suntan oil."

"That disaster I can cure," Anna said, tossing the smallest Lewis a tube of lotion. "Here. But you can only stay if you're cheerful; grumpy Lewises we have our share of."

"Rats," Cindy muttered. Picking up her surfboard, she headed back for the ocean.

"Don't scare the fish, Cindy," Duffy called after her. He received only a muffled growl in response.

When the two younger Lewis sisters arrived home, tired and slightly sunburned, they found Nicole sitting in the kitchen, drinking a cup of milky coffee.

"Any luck?" Mollie asked.

Nicole's glum expression was answer enough. "I'm not in the mood to cook," Nicole told her sisters. "You can find something in the freezer."

Cindy, pulling open the refrigerator door, shook her head. "Dibs on the last frozen pizza. What are you going to do, Nicole?"

Nicole shrugged. "Call the college again Monday and tell them I'm really stuck. Maybe they can think of something."

The mood in the Lewis household was still despondent late Sunday afternoon when Mr. and Mrs. Lewis returned. The three girls were lounging around in the family room—Cindy sprawled across the carpet with Winston draped over her legs, Mollie curled up in the big easy chair reading a teen magazine, and Nicole perched on the end of the sofa, lost in thought as she absentmindedly stroked a contented Smokey.

They all looked up as their parents came in, laughing and talking.

"Wasn't Harold funny? Who would have thought that he'd give up stockbroking to run a health farm?" Laura Lewis was saying.

"Dad!" Mollie screeched, genuinely horrified at the sight of their slightly balding father, who seemed to have suddenly acquired shoulder-length curls.

"Don't you like it?" Richard Lewis pulled off the blond wig and examined it carefully. "I thought it was just my style."

Cindy, laughing despite herself, said, "I take it the reunion was really awesome."

"We had a great time," Laura Lewis told them, sitting down on the couch beside Nicole. "So many people I haven't seen in so long. It's fascinating to see what they're doing now and where they've all scattered. One of my roommates, who never studied, finally ended up as a psychologist, for goodness' sake. And the shyest girl in the class is now a state senator in New Mexico!"

"That's nice," Nicole roused herself enough to say.

"I have former classmates living in New York, Miami, Chicago—one girl even came over from London, would you believe it?"

"Too bad you didn't find one living in Canada," Mollie said.

Her mother didn't reply. Mollie, along with the other two girls, looked up to see their mother grinning broadly, and their father trying not to chuckle.

"Mother!" Nicole jumped to her feet, sending Smokey sprawling onto the floor. "Did you? What part—not Quebec City?"

"None other!"

"Oh, Mother! *Quelle fortune!*" Nicole, afraid to believe this unexpected luck after so many disappointments, seemed to be holding her breath. "Can she find me a place to stay?"

Mrs. Lewis nodded, unable to keep her daughter in suspense any longer. "Mona's husband is a senior civil servant working in a government office in Quebec. Her daughter just left home to spend a year in France, and she said she's terribly lonesome, and would love to have guests for part of the summer."

"*Vive* reunions!" Nicole shrieked, pulling her mother into a fervent hug. "You're wonderful; your friend is wonderful; I'll be forever thankful!"

Cindy, telling herself that she was genuinely happy for her sister, couldn't quite suppress an envious sigh, as Winston barked happily, adding to the general confusion.

But Mollie, her quick ears picking up the clue Cindy had missed, broke into Nicole's excited rambling. "Did you say *guests,* Mom?"

Mrs. Lewis nodded. "Mona suggested that all three of you go. Quebec is a marvelous place, lots of history and culture, not to mention shopping, sports events, and special carnivals."

"Yow!" Mollie began to jump up and down beside her sister. Smokey, who appeared to think that *all* the humans had lost their senses, stalked off, her gray tail high in the air.

Cindy, grinning, gave her dad a bear hug. "That's great. Although—"

"Yes?" her dad prompted.

"You didn't happen to find an old college friend living in Hawaii, did you?" the eternally optimistic Lewis asked.

Chapter 4

*A*fter the impromptu celebration, Nicole made an excuse to go up to her room. Smokey, who followed her, jumped up on the Laura Ashley bedspread and pushed her way onto Nicole's lap. Nicole, deep in thought, jumped, then looked down at the gray and white cat.

"I guess I'm a real monster," she confessed, stroking the cat's soft fur. "But I really wanted to go alone; this was supposed to be my special trip, *n'est-ce pas?* And now I've got my two little sisters tagging along, like always! It's totally disgusting."

Smokey purred, apparently in complete agreement.

"But I can't tell Mother and Dad that, after Mother's friend offered to take all three of us— thank heavens she did offer, or I might have lost the whole trip. And Cindy and Mollie are so excited, how can I tell them I wish they weren't going?" Nicole stopped and frowned at her reflection in her bureau mirror. "I guess I'm stuck with them."

Smokey licked one paw complacently and began to wash her face. Nicole pushed the cat gently off her lap and went to look into her closet. "Guess I can finish packing, anyhow. Maybe—" She allowed herself one not very nice thought. "They won't be able to get plane tickets."

But the Lewis luck seemed to have changed. Last-minute cancellations allowed Mrs. Lewis to reserve two more plane tickets without any problem, and the whole Lewis family darted around like a cageful of monkeys, so their father laughingly said, in a flurry of last-minute shopping and packing.

Mollie emptied her whole closet and repacked her bags at least three times: first when Nicole pointed out that the summer temperature in Quebec, one of their northern neighbors, was going to be cooler than southern California weather; then, while Mollie was packing all of her winter sweaters, Nicole put her head through the doorway, saying, "Mollie, *mon dieu,* we're not going to live with the Eskimos!" Mollie made a face and started over again.

Cindy, watching her little sister sorting through all her clothes, added, "Don't make the same mistake you did on our camping trip, Mollie, and take three times too many clothes."

"You were glad I did when your clothes got drenched and you had to borrow some of mine," Mollie reminded her.

After that, no one gave her any more advice.

But somehow they made it to the airport on

time, gave their parents one last hug and kiss, and hurried up the stairway to the big jet.

"I can't believe it. We're really on our way," Cindy said, looking around the plane with interest.

"We're not sitting with you, Nicole." Mollie told her older sister, as she eyed the rest of the passengers, hoping for a good-looking young man in the same row. "We're in the back of the plane; Dad couldn't get our seats all together."

"That's okay," Nicole said, privately just as glad to have some time to herself. "Here, I've got a bunch of books on Quebec; do you want to read one on the plane?"

Mollie, who had already bought a new copy of *Seventeen,* shook her head, but Cindy accepted one of the books before all three girls headed for their seats. Mollie, who had never flown before, tried to disguise the tremors of nervousness that threatened to overwhelm her.

"Cindy," she murmured to her sister. "We're not going to crash, are we?"

"Of course not, shrimp," the other girl told her. "Air travel is the safest type, statistically speaking."

"I don't care about statistics," Mollie murmured, swallowing the lump in her throat. She fastened her seat belt, then had a moment of panic until she discovered how to unfasten it.

"Pull up on the end, airhead," her sister commanded, watching Mollie struggle with the recalcitrant belt.

"I was looking for a button to push," Mollie tried to sound dignified. "They're not like the seat belts in our car." She refastened her belt and tried to look blasé about her first flight.

Mollie listened wide-eyed as the stewardess went through her safety routine for the passengers. Then the plane began to taxi down the runway.

"Cindy!" Mollie gasped. "We're taking off."

"That's the idea," her sister said. "Did you think we were going to drive all the way to Canada?"

Mollie grasped her older sister's hand and gulped as the ground fell away beneath them. As the plane climbed rapidly, Mollie's stomach rolled, and she swallowed hard, forcing her ears to pop. When the aircraft attained its proper altitude and the seat-belt sign blinked off, she relaxed, beginning to feel like a veteran flier.

After she had investigated the rest of the seat controls, learned how to put her seat back and her tray table down, rented a pair of headphones from the stewardess, and found a channel that played current hits, Mollie at last lost herself in her magazine, much to Cindy's relief.

The flight to Chicago, where they had to change planes, was uneventful. But when they deplaned at the big O'Hare airport, they hit their first major snag.

"Nicole, where's our plane?" Mollie asked, after they had walked down to their designated gate.

"It should be here; we're supposed to leave again in thirty minutes," Nicole said, sounding worried. "Let me ask the man at the counter."

When she returned, Nicole was frowning. "The plane's been delayed; we'll just have to wait."

She settled down with her book, but Cindy, who had never been to Chicago and hated to miss any opportunity to see something new, persuaded Mollie to walk around the airport.

Some time later, Mollie complained, "Cindy, we must have hiked ten miles! Let's take a rest."

"What for?"

But Cindy allowed the younger girl to drag her into a gift shop where Mollie could browse through the racks. Then they both bought a hot dog and cola at a snack bar. Finally it occurred to Cindy that they'd better check on the status of their plane.

"Oh, no! What if we've missed it?" Mollie moaned.

"Hurry up, shrimp," Cindy said to her little sister, afraid to admit Mollie could be right. When they finally got back to their starting point, they discovered their plane still hadn't arrived, but an anxious Nicole wouldn't allow them to leave again.

"*Mon dieu,* I'm supposed to be in charge! You two stay put. The plane should be ready to leave soon."

The two younger Lewises sat down on the hard bench and stared at the clock. "Soon" turned out to be almost three hours later, when they finally boarded their aircraft.

"What time will we get to Quebec City, Nicole?" Mollie asked, trying to hold on to her flight bag, purse, magazine, and the stuffed bear she couldn't resist buying in the gift shop.

"I don't know. Let's just hope we can still make our connection in Montreal," Nicole worried.

Mollie, feeling like an old hand, survived another takeoff, and after a late lunch, put her seat back and went to sleep, not waking until they began to land.

"Are we in Canada yet?" she demanded, trying to peer through the twilight outside the small windows.

"Hush," Cindy hissed, seeing amused glances directed their way. "You sound like you're two years old."

Offended, Mollie kept her questions to herself. Unlike the ill-fated camping trip, this time she intended to show her sisters just how mature and responsible she could be. Not until they deplaned and were reunited with Nicole, did she venture another question.

"Now what?"

"I don't know," Nicole admitted. "It's past seven. I think we've missed our flight to Quebec City."

The flight board above their heads confirmed her fears. Nicole, trying to appear poised, stood in line to query the lady behind the counter.

She returned to her two sisters, looking even more distressed. "There isn't another flight to Quebec City until tomorrow!"

Mollie's lips quivered. "If only we hadn't been delayed in Chicago," she wailed, forgetting her pledge of maturity.

Even the dauntless Cindy looked blank. "What do we do, Nicole? Spend the night on a bench in the airport?"

"I don't know," Nicole confessed reluctantly. She had felt so grown-up, off on her first transcontinental journey. But she hadn't expected so many problems! She put down her flight bag, discovering that her shoulders ached with weariness and tension. "I'll go find a phone and call home; I'll ask Mother what we should do. You two wait here."

While Nicole strode off to the line of phones, Mollie slumped into a seat, wishing that she were home in her own bed. Traveling suddenly didn't seem like quite so much fun.

But when she returned, Nicole had regained the bounce in her step.

"Well?" Cindy asked. "What did she say?"

"First we should go back to the airline counter and confirm our flight in the morning, then find the information or travelers' aid desk, ask for the name of a hotel near the airport and the best way to get there, then call to make sure they have a room. Mother's calling Mona to tell her about our delayed arrival."

"Do we have enough money?" Cindy asked.

Nicole pulled open her purse and showed them a small piece of plastic. "Mother gave me one of her credit cards for emergencies like this."

"Oh!" Mollie perked up.

"And she told me *exactly* how much you're allowed to charge while we're gone, Mollie," Nicole said sternly.

"Oh." Mollie's face fell.

But Nicole looked more like her usual self. The younger girls followed behind as Nicole took care of the details. When the helpful lady behind the desk found them a room, and gave them directions to the bus, they all hurried to the bus stop, carrying their hand luggage.

"Nicole," Mollie exclaimed. "Where are our suitcases? I don't have any pajamas, or any clothes to wear tomorrow!"

Nicole frowned at her younger sister. "The big bags are checked through to the final destination, Mollie. What on earth have you got in that thing?"

She nodded toward the bulging flight bag that Mollie carried.

"Important things," Mollie assured her earnestly. "My make-up, curling iron, hot rollers, blow dryer—"

Nicole groaned. "Did you at least put in a toothbrush?"

Mollie looked blank.

Cindy, who had her Walkman in her bag, laughed. "Good job, shrimp."

Nicole shook her head. "Maybe you can buy one at the hotel. Hurry, there's our bus."

They took off at a run and soon were peering through the bus windows for their first close-up view of Montreal at night.

"Mon dieu," Nicole murmured. "This is so exciting; I can hardly believe I'm really here."

"Yeah, this is great," Cindy added. "If we hadn't had the delay, we'd never have gotten to spend the night in Montreal."

Nicole's smile was wide. *"C'est vrai.* And as soon as we check into the hotel, I'm going out. I'm not wasting this opportunity!"

"What about us?" Mollie demanded.

"You can go to bed."

Mollie sulked, but Cindy gave her sister a surreptitious wink, and Mollie felt better. Cindy had something planned, too!

Chapter 5

*T*he hotel was modern and attractive. They checked in without problems, Nicole signed all the forms, and the girls soon arrived in their room, where they inspected the double bed and roll-away cot that had been delivered to accommodate their last-minute request.

"Who gets the roll-away?" Cindy asked.

"I'll take it," Nicole offered nobly.

Cindy looked surprised but pleased, then said, "Hey, that means I have to sleep with Mollie! She kicks!"

Mollie threw her sisters a dirty look, then went to investigate the bathroom. She called from inside the other room, "Nicole, what's a *rince-bouche*?"

"What?" Nicole and Cindy hurried to look over Mollie's shoulder as she inspected the toiletries laid out beside the washbasin. "Oh, that's mouth wash."

"In French, how cute," Mollie giggled. "And here's a *bonnet de douche*—a shower cap. I love it!"

It was true that seeing ordinary amenities labeled in a different language made their trip seem even more exciting. "This is a real adventure," Mollie told herself as she brushed her thick blond hair. "Our Quebec adventure!"

When Mollie came out of the bathroom, Nicole was skimming one of her much-thumbed guidebooks. "I can't decide what I want to see most—trying to decide from all of Montreal when I only have a few hours is maddening!"

"And you're really going to leave us to sit in the hotel room?" Mollie protested, her sense of injustice making her ignore Cindy's meaningful look. "That's not fair!"

"*Mon dieu*, I'm not going to waste this unexpected opportunity looking out for a couple of kids!" Nicole's pent-up frustration made her blunt. "You two call room service and order a sandwich, then watch TV or go to bed. Just stay out of trouble!" The eldest Lewis disappeared into the bathroom, leaving Mollie steaming with rebellion.

"Cindy," she demanded. "We're not going to take this lying down, are we?"

"Of course not, shrimp," Cindy assured her little sister. "Just keep your mouth shut until Nicole's gone."

So when Nicole opened the door, her make-up redone and her soft brown hair combed, she found her two siblings in a suspiciously acquiescent mood. She was in too much of a hurry to think about it now; precious time was passing.

"Don't be mad, Mollie," she told the youngest Lewis. "I'll make it up to you when we get to Quebec City, *je te promets.*"

Mollie shrugged. Nicole grabbed her sweater and shut the door behind her.

They waited a moment to make sure she had made it to the elevator, then jumped up from the foot of the bed.

"Now what?" Mollie demanded eagerly. "Where are we going, Cindy?"

"There's something special I want to see," Cindy told her.

"What? A shopping center?"

Cindy gave her sister a glance of pure disdain; Mollie tried again. "An amusement park?"

Cindy shook her head.

Mollie searched her mind, and paled. "Surely you don't want to go to a museum?"

Cindy hooted. "I'm not Nicole! No, Mollie, there's something in Montreal I've always wanted to try."

"What?" Mollie's eyes widened.

Cindy, a true child of southern California, grinned. "Montreal has a terrific subway!"

Meanwhile, Nicole stopped in the lobby to ask for directions, took a short bus ride, and soon found herself looking up at the towering facade of the Chateau Champlain Hotel. She made her way inside, located the bank of elevator doors, and soon, gulping at the quick ascent, stepped off at the thirty-sixth floor. Here, as her guidebook had promised, the L'Escapade supper club awaited; but Nicole ignored the seated patrons and the soft murmur of conversation, spellbound by the breathtaking view.

Floor to ceiling semicircular windows looked out over downtown Montreal; the city, lights bright against the dark evening sky, presented an awe-inspiring sight. Nicole, speechless with wonder as she admired the glittering skyscrapers, forgot everything in delighted admiration of the skyline. A discreet waiter finally caught her attention.

"Madame would like a table, yes?"

"Yes, I mean, *oui, s'il vous plait.*"

Once Nicole was settled at a quiet table by one of the windows, she ordered a glass of iced tea. When the tall glass arrived, she took a sip, never taking her eyes off the panorama of city lights beyond the windows.

When the waiter returned, Nicole, despite the restaurant's excellent reputation, was too restless to stay. She had to visit at least one more famous night spot before she returned to the hotel; this one night had to be stretched as far as possible.

On the way out, she spotted a public telephone, and her conscience prompted a quick call to the hotel, to check on her sisters.

When the hotel operator answered, Nicole gave her the room number and waited while the phone rang unheeded. At last admitting that no one was going to answer, Nicole replaced the receiver, her smooth forehead wrinkled with worry.

"They probably decided to go down to the coffee shop," she murmured to herself. "They're not babies, after all. I am *not* going to ruin my evening worrying about them!"

But as she headed back to the elevator, Nicole felt anxiety growing in the back of her mind.

Cindy and Mollie, directed by the friendly personnel in the hotel lobby, easily found a subway station.

"Wow," Mollie breathed, examining a huge mosaic, bright and attractive, that hung over the train track where it disappeared into a tunnel. "This looks like an art museum; I thought subways were dark and dirty and covered with graffiti."

"That's just in New York," Cindy told her wisely.

"And when were you in New York, smarty?" her sister demanded.

"I've seen lots of movies," Cindy answered, undaunted. "Here, put your dollar down this little chute. I'm glad we changed some money at the hotel."

They passed the ticket-seller's booth, and, aided by another passenger's example, found the machine that gave out free transfers.

"How far are we going?" Mollie asked, admiring the sleek lines of the modern blue train as it swept into the station. Now that she'd stopped worrying about being mugged—she'd seen some of those movies, too—Mollie was having fun.

"Who knows?" Cindy grinned. "Come on."

They boarded the train, admired the soundless doors, the comfortable interior, and the swift ride.

"Here's the Viau station," announced Cindy, after consulting her guidebook. "Come on, this is where we get off."

"Where are we going?" Mollie hurried to keep up with her sister.

"They've got an Olympic stadium here that was built for the Montreal Olympics in 1976. I've seen amazing pictures of it," Cindy enthused.

"I should have known," Mollie said with a groan.

Much to Cindy's disappointment, and Mollie's secret relief, they were too late for the last guided tour and only got a glimpse of the giant oval stadium that could seat eighty-thousand people. Cindy, acknowledging defeat, led the way back to the subway.

"Let's get something to eat; I'm starved," she told the younger Lewis.

"Good idea," Mollie agreed. "Where? Back at the hotel?"

"No way." Cindy shook her head. "We're not going back so soon. Listen to this, Mollie. Montreal has an underground city!"

"Like ants?"

"I'm serious; you can take the Metro to all sorts of places—theaters, boutiques—"

"Really?" Mollie brightened at once.

"Restaurants—over a hundred to choose from," Cindy finished firmly. "All we have to do is take our pick."

They made their way back to the Berri-de-Montigny station, where several subway lines crossed, and Cindy picked out a new direction. Unfortunately, once they were seated on the new car, Cindy put her head back into her guidebook, and Mollie spotted a good-looking guy at the end of the train. By the time she had thought of a way to start a conversation, and was happily filling him in on life in Santa Barbara, Cindy suddenly looked up. "Darn, we've gone past our station!" she exclaimed.

"Oh, Cindy," Mollie wailed. "Are we lost?"

"Of course not," her sister said. "We'll just have to get out and go back the other way. Come on."

The Café de Paris, at the Hotel Ritz-Carlton, was a renowned and expensive restaurant, but after all, Nicole told herself a little guiltily, she was only in Montreal for one night. Although she knew she'd have many opportunities in Quebec City, Nicole was impatient to try some really top-notch French cuisine. She waited for the maître-d' and admired the quiet elegance of her surroundings as she was shown to a small table.

When an attractive waiter presented her with a menu, Nicole found herself overwhelmed with delightful choices.

"Je ne sais pas," she murmured.

The waiter was happy to assist her. "Perhaps Mademoiselle should start with the galantine of pheasant *aux chanterelles*?"

"Oh, yes."

"Excellent choice," the man nodded. "Then venison, perhaps, or the fresh Atlantic salmon? And the *tourment d'amour*—coconut cake flavored with rum—to finish?"

"It sounds heavenly," Nicole sighed happily. She placed her order, then, when the waiter departed, glanced around at her fellow diners: the men in dark suits and ties, the women in sleek, fashionable gowns. This was definitely living, Nicole thought happily.

Then a false note marred the harmony of this special evening. Nicole remembered her sisters. *"Mon dieu,"* she told herself. "I'd better call again; they're surely back in the hotel room by now."

She slipped away from her table, found the ladies' room and a public phone, and called the hotel. She waited while the operator rang their room and listened as the phone again rang unheeded. Nicole finally replaced the receiver after the tenth ring.

Nicole glanced at her watch. Nine o'clock. Suddenly all sorts of terrible visions filled her head. "Where on earth can they be at this hour? Surely they didn't leave the hotel—"

She suddenly remembered how easily Mollie had given in, and how Cindy hadn't argued with her at all. "Those rats—" she gasped. "They were planning to go out all along. And alone in a big city. *Mon dieu,* where could they have gone?"

She couldn't sit still and enjoy a leisurely dinner, no matter how renowned the chef, if her two younger sisters were lost in the darkness of big-city streets.

"I should have come to Quebec by myself, I just knew it," Nicole said crossly, as she made a hurried and embarrassed excuse to the waiter and headed for the bus stop. "Whatever will they do next?"

By the time they found the correct station,

even Cindy was getting her fill of subway, so both girls felt better when Cindy could declare, "Here we are, Mollie. The underground city!"

"Good grief." Mollie looked around, wide-eyed. "This is incredible. Look at those terrific clothes in that shop window."

"No way." Cindy took a firm hold on her younger sister. "I'm starved. How about some Chinese?"

Mollie looked doubtful. "Shouldn't we eat something French?"

Cindy snorted. "You sound like Nicole. Montreal's a very cosmopolitan city, and besides, I feel like egg rolls."

They entered the Chinese restaurant, made their way to a red booth, ordered from a waiter in black trousers and white shirt, and soon were stuffing themselves with an array of Chinese dishes.

"That was good," Mollie had to admit when they were done. "Now what? Back to the hotel?"

"Let's explore a little," Cindy suggested.

Mollie, yawning, looked dubious.

"There are some great shops here."

"You convinced me." Mollie woke up at once.

They paid their bill and wandered along the well-lit underground streets. Mollie would have browsed happily for hours, but Cindy, soon bored by window-shopping, kept dragging her sister on.

"Wow!" Cindy exclaimed. "Look, Mollie, a swimming pool!"

Mollie, who had been about to make up her mind on a particularly stunning sweater, looked sulky. "It's too late to go swimming."

Cindy ignored her, stopping to inspect the menu

posted outside another restaurant. "Look, Mollie, this one's Greek. What do you suppose *avgolemono* soup is? or *tzatziki* dip?"

"We just ate, Cindy."

"Just an appetizer," Cindy argued, her usual curiosity too strong to ignore. "Come on."

Sighing, Mollie followed her sister inside. Later, Cindy's culinary knowledge expanded to her satisfaction, Mollie said, "That's enough; I'm stuffed!"

"Me, too," Cindy said, just as she spotted a small Hungarian restaurant with a tray of desserts promptly displayed in the window.

"Cindy!" Mollie warned.

"But just look at those pastries!"

Mollie looked, and gave up. "Just a small one," she warned, and they plunged inside the restaurant.

Even Cindy was beginning to feel her belt tighten by the time they left this restaurant, and Mollie moaned, "I'll leave Quebec as fat as a suckling pig."

Cindy laughed. "Don't sweat it, shrimp. We'll walk back to the station. I guess we'd better get back to the hotel; it's getting pretty late."

Mollie, checking her watch, looked apprehensive. It was ten o'clock. "Nicole will kill us!"

"Maybe she's not back yet, either," Cindy said hopefully. "Anyhow, we'll be back at the hotel in a jiffy."

And they might have been, if Cindy hadn't somehow managed to forget which station they had to disembark from. When they climbed the stairs to the street entrance, the two girls looked around, dismayed.

"This isn't our hotel," Mollie blurted, her eyes wide. "We're lost, Cindy!"

"Relax," Cindy said, trying to think. "Look, that delicatessen is still open. We'll go in and ask for directions."

Not only did they get cheerful instructions, but Cindy, glimpsing the array of food behind the counter, wavered.

"No more food!" Mollie argued. "I'm going to burst!"

"But smell—" Cindy sniffed appreciatively. "Just a little of that smoked meat, with a kosher pickle on the side."

Mollie groaned.

When they finally reached their hotel and made their way up to their room, Cindy unlocked the door very quietly, in the vain hope that Nicole might be asleep. They found a furious Lewis lying in wait for them.

"Where on earth have you two been? I've been worried sick; I called the police twice!"

"You did?" Cindy murmured, impressed despite herself. Mollie looked ready to cry at this evidence of Nicole's concern. "What did they say?"

"They told me Montreal is a very safe city, and you would probably turn up soon," Nicole admitted. But her anger still flared. "Where did you go?"

"Just went out for a bite to eat," Cindy hedged, then gave up. "Darn it, Nicole, what did you expect us to do? Sit in a hotel room while you were out having fun? We rode on the Metro and saw the underground city—we had a great time."

Mollie, who hadn't spoken a word, threw a beseeching glance at her older sister, then darted for the bathroom.

"Mollie's positively green—what's wrong?" Nicole asked, her irritation beginning to subside.

Cindy, who according to family jokes possessed an iron stomach, shrugged. "Who knows—it might have been the egg rolls—or the Greek soup—or the Viennesse pastry, or maybe the pickles."

Nicole threw up her hands and dropped to the bed, not sure whether to laugh or cry. "You two ate your way across Montreal, and I never even had my dinner! *Quelle mauvaise chance!*"

Chapter 6

*T*he girls' flight to Quebec City left early the next morning and there were no more unexpected problems. The Lewis sisters found Mona Gilbert, alerted to the change in plans by a call from Mrs. Lewis, waiting at the airport.

"Bonjour, mes enfants!" she greeted them. "Welcome to Quebec at last! You must be Nicole—how very like your mother you are."

Nicole, warming at once to this tall stately woman with the friendly smile and stylish clothes, smiled and nodded.

"And this is Cindy—yes? And the *petite jeune fille* is Mollie."

Mollie, her eyes wide, exclaimed impulsively, "How did you know?"

"Ah, your mother described you all very well."

"Mrs.—Madame Gilbert, are you American or Canadian?" Cindy blurted.

A stern look from Nicole reminded her that this was perhaps a more personal question than should have been directed to their hostess, but the tall woman laughed and answered readily.

"A little of both. My mother was from Quebec and she married a Californian who was working in Montreal. When she died, my father went back to California and later remarried, and I, of course, went with him. But after college, I grew homesick for my birthplace and sought a position here. Then, when I married Henri, I knew that this was really my home."

"How romantic," Mollie sighed.

Cindy, pretending to adjust the flight bag hung over her shoulder, managed to elbow her younger sister, which effectively broke the spell. Mollie glared, but kept her mouth shut while Nicole plied Madame Gilbert with eager questions.

After they had retrieved their baggage and piled into Madame Gilbert's small sedan, the short ride to her home was punctuated by exclamations from all three girls.

"Oh, look." Mollie stared through the car window. "The front door is on the second floor." She pointed to a wrought-iron staircase that led up to the main door of the old residence, and her sisters turned to look.

"This is all so—so French!" Nicole murmured, and the other two girls, accustomed to their Francophile sister, exchanged resigned glances. They continued to admire the attractive homes with their gray stone gabled roofs until they reached their destination.

The Gilbert home was spacious and attractive. The girls carried their luggage upstairs, where Madame Gilbert showed them to a large, pleasant room, with windows framed in white lace and two comfortable beds hidden by fluffy white coverlets. She left them to settle in and went to check on the noontime meal, already hinted at by savory odors drifting through the house.

"Isn't this wonderful?" Nicole said, dropping down on the wide bed, overcome with delight now that they were finally in Quebec City.

Cindy viewed the two beds with misgivings. "Does this mean I get stuck sleeping with Mollie *again*?"

"We'll draw straws," Nicole offered generously, refusing to allow her perfect mood to be blighted.

Mollie threw them both a haughty look and opened her suitcase. Cindy and Nicole followed her example. By the time most of their unpacking was completed, a call from the stairway summoned them to lunch.

"*Vite,* girls," their hostess called.

"What's that?" Cindy asked.

"It means 'quickly,'" Mollie told her sister, feeling very knowledgeable now that she had one year of French behind her. "Don't worry, Cindy; I'll translate for you."

Cindy grunted, not sure that she was going to like being the only Lewis who didn't speak French. "I don't know about this foreign language stuff."

"We're the foreigners here, idiot," Nicole spoke sharply. "Just remember that we're guests in this country, and mind your manners."

Cindy made a face at her elder sister, but they all hurried down to the dining room. After a delicious meal, Madame Gilbert offered to show them around the city, but Nicole refused politely.

"We don't want to be a bother," she said.

Madame Gilbert smiled. "Ah, well," she said. "I know you'll enjoy wandering around on your own. Dinner is at six."

They promised not to be late, and armed with a walking map, and—at Madame Gilbert's insistence—a written notation of their hostess's address and enough money for taxi fare, just in case, the three girls hurried out.

Nicole decided that they should start their tour with a visit to the Citadel. As they walked, she kept up a running commentary. "The name Quebec comes from an Indian word, *kebec,* meaning place where the river narrows. When Cartier first sailed up the Saint-Laurent, he saw the cliffs of Cape Diamond and called it the Gilbraltar of the North. But it was Champlain who started the first settlement."

Mollie interrupted this monologue, exclaiming, "Wow, look at that place. Why the walls, Nicole? Did someone attack the city?"

"Just about everybody," Nicole said. "The Indians, in the beginning, then the English, even the United States."

"We did?" Mollie looked startled.

"Benedict Arnold led an attack in 1775; he didn't succeed; the English did."

They were too late to see the changing of the guard, but, along with a horde of fellow tourists, they admired the colorful uniforms. Then the Lewis sisters decided to eschew the guided tour and wander through the great structure on their own. Nicole, overflowing with information, continued to lecture her sisters. "Down there, southwest of the city on the Plains of Abraham is where the British forces, led by General Wolfe, fought the French, commanded by the Marquis de Montcalm in 1759."

"And the French won," Mollie said wisely.

"Mais non!" Nicole threw her sister a disdainful glance. "Don't you remember anything you learned in school? The English won, although both generals died from wounds suffered during the battle."

"So why do they still speak French?" Cindy asked.

"Because even though Britain controlled the Canadian provinces, the French settlers didn't give up their language, or culture," Nicole told them, looking superior. "And today both French and English are official languages in Canada. But outside of the Province of Quebec, most Canadians speak English as their first language."

She would have continued the commentary but Cindy was examining a large iron cannon, and Mollie had paused to smile encouragingly at a dark-haired teenager wearing a Princeton T-shirt.

Nicole sighed. "Come on, you uncultured savages," she commanded.

After they had examined the great fortress enough to satisfy Nicole, and admired the view, Mollie noticed a beautiful building and gasped, "What's that, Nicole? It looks like Cinderella's castle!"

Nicole stared at the great turreted structure that dominated a cliff overlooking the river. "That's the Chateau Frontenac," she told them. "It was named after the Comte de Frontenac, one of New France's most famous governors. A world-famous hotel, it has five-hundred rooms. Churchill and Roosevelt conferred there during World War II; Queen Elizabeth, and tons of other royalty, have stayed there."

"I feel like I've wandered into a fairy tale," Mollie sighed. "Now what?"

"Let's find the *Funiculaire*," Nicole told them, "and we'll go down to the Lower Town."

"What's that?"

"Sort of a cross between an elevator and a cable car," Nicole told them.

They soon located the station, and enjoyed the descent in the glass-walled funicular. There was so much to see that Nicole could hardly choose which sight to admire first. After several more hours of sightseeing, the younger girls' energy began to wane.

"Let's get something to drink, Nicole," Mollie suggested. "All this walking has left me dry as a bone."

"Good idea," Cindy agreed.

Even Nicole, lured by the colorful sidewalk cafés with their bright umbrellas and small, crowded tables, found the idea enticing. They finally found an empty table and sank into narrow chairs with a sigh of relief.

"My poor feet," Mollie slipped her feet out of her fashionable, if overly tight shoes and wriggled her toes.

"It's your own fault," Cindy, said, pointing her own toes in her worn comfortable running shoes.

When Nicole ordered, the waiter blinked for a moment, then shrugged and departed.

"Nicole," Cindy said, "are you sure he understood you?"

"Why shouldn't he?" Nicole asked, bristling at any slight to her command of French.

"Okay, if you say so," Cindy gave in. They waited, watching other people stroll along the narrow street, until the waiter returned, followed by an older man in a neat blue jacket.

"There is some problem?" he asked, in heavily accented English.

"*Non, non,*" Nicole assured him.

The man spoke again in French, and Nicole, turning red, answered quickly. Her two sisters, watching, were completely mystified.

"What's wrong?" Mollie demanded.

"Nothing," Nicole murmured, and the man, his expression amused, turned away from the table. The waiter served their drinks, and Mollie sipped her cola, but Cindy refused to be put off.

"Come on, Nicole, what was that all about? What did you do?"

"I only ordered coffee, *café au lait,*" Nicole, still looking embarrassed, murmured. "But the waiter thought that I asked for the *cafetier,* the café owner."

Cindy almost fell off her chair laughing, and even Mollie succumbed to a fit of giggling.

"Our sister, the expert," Cindy gasped, when she could catch her breath.

"Shut up!" Nicole whispered, conscious of amused looks from the patrons sitting at the tables around them. "The accent here is different, that's all. I'll get used to it soon. It's more than you can do!"

"I don't know," Cindy quipped. "I think my Spanish would do as much good as your French."

Nicole's answering look was murderous; an incipient argument was prevented only by Mollie, whose mind had wandered to other things. "Look at that pastry!" she interrupted. "Can I have a piece, Nicole, please?"

"You don't want to spoil your dinner," Nicole told her, in her best older-sister tone.

But Mollie's glance was beseeching. "I'm hungry enough to eat the whole menu; just one piece, Nicole?"

"Me, too," Cindy agreed.

"Oh, all right."

Mollie ordered, by the simple method of pointing to the dessert that had tempted her, and soon both Lewises were enjoying the flaky torte.

"Delicious," Mollie said happily.

"I'm going to find the ladies' room; I'll be right back," Nicole told them.

"If all the food is this good, I'll gain twenty pounds before we go home," Mollie worried.

Cindy shook her head. "Don't worry. if Nicole has her way, she'll walk it off us."

Mollie, consoled, finished her dessert. When the waiter returned to take away their plates, she smiled and patted her stomach. "I'm full—I mean—" she tried to remember her limited French vocabulary—*"je suis plein."*

The waiter looked startled, and behind them, a motherly woman at the next table clucked in dismay. "How sad—and so young, too," she said to her companion.

Mollie, bewildered, looked at Cindy, who shrugged. But Nicole, just arriving back at the table, overheard the exchange. Red-faced, she grabbed Mollie by the arm and hissed, "Come on!"

"But Nicole," Mollie protested, as they hurried away from the little café. "All I said was that I was full. Why did everyone stare at me?"

Nicole groaned. "That's what you tried to say, Mollie. What you told them was that you're pregnant."

"What?" Mollie shrieked.

Cindy, once again overcome with laughter, fell off the curb.

Nicole threw up her hands in despair. "I'm not sure Quebec is ready for you two! Come on, before we cause a scandal."

They made a quick exit, with Cindy, still chuckling, in tow.

Chapter 7

*M*onday *morning Nicole was the first of the* three sisters out of bed, beating even Cindy, who was usually the earliest riser. Nervous at the prospect of her first day of class, Nicole had slept restlessly, despite the comfortable bed, and she woke as the first timid rays of sunlight lightened the dark sky.

She got up and dressed quietly, then sat down with one of her French textbooks, trying to refresh a memory that seemed to have gone abruptly blank.

Cindy, sitting up in the other bed, her short blond hair tousled from sleep, stared at her sister. "What are you doing up so early?"

"Just looking through some notes," Nicole replied.

Cindy frowned. "For Pete's sake, Nicole, you were Madame Preston's best pupil; you'll float through this class."

Nicole shook her head. "This is not your average high school class, Cindy. These people are *all* outstanding students."

"You'll still be the star of the class," Cindy predicted confidently, pushing herself out of bed. The lump on the other side of the mattress stirred sleepily, complaining, "Why is everyone so noisy?" Mollie struggled to open her blue eyes, blinking in bewilderment as she looked around the room until her memory returned.

"We're in Quebec!" She sat up abruptly, as if anxious not to lose a moment of their stay in this fascinating province.

"Give the girl a gold star," Cindy said.

They all went down the staircase together and walked into the sunny dining room, where the white-clothed table with its small vase of fresh flowers made an attractive picture.

"Anyone for croissants?" Madame Gilbert offered, smiling at them. Nicole nodded, as she greeted Monsieur Gilbert.

"Sleep well?" he asked, folding up the newspaper as he rose from the table.

"Yes, thank you," Nicole told him. "It's a lovely morning."

"You begin your class today, yes?"

"Yes, sir," Nicole nodded.

"Bonne chance, my dear," he said kindly aas he collected his briefcase and paused to give his wife a good-bye kiss. "I'm sure you'll do very well."

Nicole, stirring her cup of café au lait, wasn't so sure. She couldn't even enjoy the flaky croissants, spread with butter and strawberry jam, with her stomach knotted with worry. While her sisters stuffed themselves on the fresh pastry, and Mollie poured over one of their guidebooks, Nicole's thoughts were far away. Finally she looked at her watch and excused herself, taking her dishes to the kitchen.

"I've got to run or I'll miss the bus. I'll see you this afternoon. Cindy, Mollie, stay out of trouble."

Mollie blinked innocent blue eyes at her sister, and Cindy looked insulted. "We're not babes in the wood," she called after her sister. "Honestly," she told Mollie. "Nicole acts like we're ten years old!"

To illustrate her maturity, Cindy picked up the rest of the breakfast dishes and carried them to the kitchen.

"Can we help with the dishes?" she asked Madame Gilbert.

"This is your vacation, *ma petite,*" their hostess protested.

"But we really want to help," Cindy told her. "It's the least we can do."

Mollie, recalled to her social responsibilities, hurried to help her sister, and together they finished cleaning up quickly. As soon as they were done, Mollie picked up the guidebook.

"Where to today?" she asked.

"I don't know," Cindy answered. "I would have loved to have seen some ice-hockey games. The Canadians really excel at that sport, you know."

Madame Gilbert nodded and said, "Ah—hockey, that is *the* national pastime. But it's the wrong time of year, Cindy. Winter is the best time for hockey games."

"Too bad," Cindy said. "I've always wanted to try it myself; it looks like quite a game."

"Mais oui," their hostess agreed. "But dangerous, too, *ma petite.* Better leave it to the boys."

Mollie opened her mouth to warn Madame Gilbert that her advice was only guaranteed to provoke the hot-tempered Cindy. But, although Cindy frowned, Mollie saw that this time her good manners prevailed.

Cindy, who had been an excellent athlete all of her life, thought rebelliously, Surfing isn't exactly a sport for sissies! Feeling unable to argue with the woman who had been so kind and hospitable, she managed to keep her peace, though not without a struggle.

"Hockey is very popular with the young, but in the summer, most of the children turn to soccer or"—Madame Gilbert smiled—"baseball. You might find some games going on in the park, Cindy."

Cindy thanked Madame Gilbert as politely as she could, but even though she enjoyed both soccer and baseball, she still had a lingering desire to try her skill on skates, something she'd only done a few times in the past.

Mollie, meanwhile, was flipping through their guidebook. "Listen to this, Cindy," she read aloud, enthusiasm obvious in her tone. "In the heart of Quebec City, the epitome of chic—the Place Quebec, with seventy-five boutiques and restaurants!"

Cindy groaned.

Nicole, meanwhile, had located the address she had been given, and after some difficulty, found the entrance to the complex of old buildings. She made her way through wrought-iron gates, pausing as she looked around the inner quadrangle.

The quiet serenity of the courtyard delighted her; gray-stone buildings, mellow with age, were topped by blue roofs with gabled windows. Nicole examined an arched window more closely.

Then a voice spoke from behind her, breaking the spell.

"*Pardon,* are you lost?"

"This is the university, *n'est-ce pas?*" Nicole fumbled with her notebook, a little flustered by the other girl's direct gaze.

"It is the Quebec Seminary; Laval University, which once occupied these buildings, moved to a new campus years ago. There are only a few classes still held here," the dark-haired girl, who had an expressive gamine's face, explained. She turned to go, but Nicole waved her slip of paper.

"This is where I was told to come; I'm looking for the honors course in French literature."

"Ah, you are one of the foreign students, yes?"

"I'm from California," Nicole answered rather stiffly.

The girl shrugged. "As I said. Come, I'll show you; I am also a student in that course."

She led the way inside one of the buildings, and Nicole hurried after her, wishing she had time to examine the brass ornaments and gilt-framed portraits that adorned the wall. But she had to be on time to class!

"My name is Nicole Lewis," she offered.

The other girl nodded. "Gabriella Gauthier."

Nicole fought to suppress a growing panic. If all the other students were French-speaking natives, this class might be difficult indeed! "Are you from Quebec?" she asked timidly.

The other girl nodded. "Joliette."

They aproached a classroom, and Gabriella gestured toward it. Nicole, her heart beating fast, entered and found most of the students already assembled. She quickly slipped into a desk, and opened her notebook. Just then the class quieted as the professor, a small man with a neat beard, walked to the front of the room. He placed his books upon the lectern, gave the seated class one sweeping glance from beneath heavy eyebrows, and said crisply, *"Bonjour."*

The professor opened his book and began speaking rapidly in French.

Nicole, gulping, began to take notes.

When Cindy could no longer bear Mollie's constant repetitions of "Look at this terrific sweater," or "Cindy, come see this beautiful bracelet—this Indian jewelry is gorgeous!," she made sure that her little sister knew how to get back to Madame Gilbert's house, and set out on her own.

She had read in one of Nicole's guidebooks that tourists could buy a tape cassette to direct them on a walking tour, so first she located the office near the Place d'Armes and purchased a cassette to slip into her always handy Walkman.

This kept her busy for an hour, and then Cindy decided to examine the *Musée Historique* on the rue Ste. Anne. This was a wax museum, more to Cindy's liking than the art museums that Nicole loved to frequent. Lifelike exhibitions such as one of Iroquois torturing a Jesuit priest held her interest for some time, but finally Cindy found herself back on the street, tired of sightseeing and wishing for a more active pursuit. After buying some postcards, she wrote brief messages to her parents and friends back home. Unable to decide which picture was most exciting, she mailed Grant two; it was nice to be able to send *him* a card from an exotic locale! Then her growling stomach reminded Cindy that it was lunchtime.

After mailing her cards, she found a small café with an empty chair and seated herself, frowning over the menu. Without Nicole or Mollie to help her, interpreting the menu could be a challenge, especially if she were in the mood for something tried and true.

"It would help if I could read the menu," she told the waiter hovering over her.

"Pardon?" The young man raised his brows, and Cindy sighed.

"Pizza, at least I know what that is." She pointed to an item on the menu. "But what's *la pizza avec fromage, tomate?*"

The waiter looked blank, but a dark-haired boy at the next table answered her in a lightly accented English. "Pizza with cheese and tomato," he explained.

"What happened to pepperoni?" Cindy, who was tired and somewhat cross, didn't stop to thank the fellow diner for his help.

"Try *la pizze garnie*," he advised.

"What's that?" Cindy muttered, not very graciously. "Oh." For the first time she discovered the English translations on the other side of the menu, but feeling foolish didn't improve her temper. "Pizza all dressed? Sounds like it's wearing high heels and a hat. Dumb!"

The boy flushed, and several other diners regarded her sternly. Cindy, remembering that she'd assured Nicole that she would not get into trouble, realized belatedly that this was *not* exactly the best way to demonstrate diplomacy in a foreign country. She stopped her grumbling and ordered the pizza, and wasn't even cheered when it turned out to be delicious.

She paid her bill and wandered down several more side streets, not sure what to do with her afternoon. Mollie had her shops and Nicole her class; both were happy and absorbed. But what about her? Then, rounding another corner, Cindy suddenly brightened. A poster on a side street advertised a sports complex, and—surely that was an indoor ice rink pictured! Maybe she could at least try her skill at ice skating. That would give her an excellent way to work off her excess energy and present her with a new challenge to boot!

She carefully noted the address and hurried off to find a bus stop. Within an hour, she had located the modern complex and found the entrance to the rink. Next she rented a pair of skates with a good deal of pantomime and the help of a friendly old gentleman in the ticket booth.

Cindy sat down on a bench and began to lace up her skates, wishing she'd brought along a sweatshirt. The rink was almost deserted, and she couldn't wait to take a spin around the smooth ice.

But she'd forgotten that ice skating wasn't quite as simple as it appeared. She took one confident step forward, and her ankles collapsed, sending her plummeting to the cold surface.

Darn! A tiny skater, hardly big enough to reach Cindy's waist, skimmed by on the ice, giggling at her ungraceful sprawl. Her cheeks burning, Cindy pulled herself to the side of the rink, grasped the rail, and managed to stand erect, ready to try again.

After an hour of practice, Cindy, a natural athlete, had remembered enough of her long-ago session on skates to be able to skate fairly confidently around the rink. But, now that she felt secure on her skates, she began to wish for a new challenge. Now what? Skating in circles was not what she'd had in mind, and fancy twirls didn't interest her.

"I wish I could try my hand at hockey," Cindy said aloud, as she practiced a smooth stop on the almost empty ice. "I bet I wouldn't be so bad."

"You?" The sudden laughter behind her made Cindy turn too quickly; she had to fight to keep her balance. Her undignified double take didn't exactly help; the boy continued to chuckle.

To Cindy's chagrin, she recognized the boy from the sidewalk café. If she hadn't been angry already, she might have tried a little harder to be polite. But being laughed at by a boy her own age who stood on his skates as if they were an extension of his long legs, didn't add to her self control.

"What's so funny about that?" she demanded.

"You can barely stand erect on the ice, *américaine.*" He grinned good-naturedly, but his words carried their own sting. "Canadians are the best at hockey; do you think you could compete with our players?"

"For your information, I'm not such a bad athlete," Cindy managed to say in a controlled voice as she struggled with her temper. When the boy raised his brows in mock surprise, she lost her fragile hold completely.

"Americans are good athletes, too, you know! If I had a chance to play, I'd show you."

She knew that her taunt sounded childish, but Cindy, accustomed to doing well in all her sports, felt that her honor had been challenged. Not just her personal honor, either! She had to stand up for her country, didn't she?

To her irritation, the teenager continued to regard her with more amusement than anger. "If you're so anxious to play, come early tomorrow morning to the back of the arena, and ask for me, Roland. Old Jacques allows us to practice before the rink opens to the public. We'll give you a chance to learn all about hockey."

"Really?" Cindy almost forgot her anger in her enthusiasm over this unexpected opportunity. But then she saw the gleam of amusement in Roland's eye and suspected that he was looking forward to seeing the brash American fall flat on her posterior.

Fine. She'd show him!

Chapter 8

*O*n Tuesday morning Cindy rose early to get in a brisk morning jog. When she returned, Mollie was still sleeping peacefully, but Nicole had already dressed and departed.

"Wake up, shrimp," Cindy commanded. She collected her clothes and headed for the bathroom as Mollie, groaning, pushed back the covers.

When they descended the staircase together, the only person still in the dining room was Madame Gilbert, who smiled and wished them good morning.

"Has Nicole left already?" Mollie asked, looking a little disturbed.

"Mais oui," their hostess told them. "She said she wanted to get to school early. Very commendable, such dedication to one's studies."

Madame Gilbert went into the kitchen for a fresh platter of eggs and bacon, and Mollie took the opportunity to whisper to her sister, "What's with Nicole? She barely said two words to us last night, burying herself in her books, and now she's gone already."

Cindy shrugged, trying to look indifferent, but she, too, felt hurt. "Nicole's pretty caught up in this class. You know that."

"But doesn't she care about us anymore?" Mollie bit her lip. "It's bad enough that she's leaving for college in a couple of months; I didn't think she would forget about us so soon!"

Cindy thought about how to respond to her younger sister as she poured herself a cup of thick cocoa. She, too, felt wounded over Nicole's avoidance of the two of them, perhaps even more so because she had a shrewd suspicion that Nicole hadn't really wanted her two younger sisters tagging along on this trip.

"Who cares?" she said brusquely, refusing to admit her concern.

Mollie sighed, but brightened a little as Madame Gilbert brought in their breakfast. Cindy, biting into a piece of toast, soon forgot about her older sister's apparent abandonment. She had the upcoming hockey practice to think about, and she quickly finished her breakfast, quietly prodding Mollie into clearing the table and doing the dishes so that she could hurry off to catch her bus.

As Mollie carried the breakfast dishes into the kitchen, she noticed Madame Gilbert, dicing vegetables on a wooden chopping block with an easy efficiency that reminded Mollie of her own mother.

"What are you making?" Mollie asked shyly.

Madame Gilbert smiled. "Cream of asparagus

soup," she explained. "I'm going to make a salmon mousse, too. Would you like to help?"

Mollie realized with a pang how much she missed her mother and the sudden homesick feeling made her think helping out in the kitchen would be a very pleasant way to spend the morning.

"Could I?"

Madame Gilbert directed her to a pantry where Mollie took down an extra apron, tied it on, and went happily to work.

When Cindy reached the ice-skating rink, the front doors were locked as Roland said they would be. She went around to the rear entrance and found the small group of hockey players suiting up.

"So, you still are eager to play the game?" the dark-haired boy she had met yesterday challenged.

"Of course," Cindy told him.

"I warn you, *américaine*, hockey is not a game for girls—it can be dangerous."

He might as well have waved a red flag in front of the volatile Lewis. "You just point me to the ice!" she told him. "I'm not worried about a few spills."

The boys exchanged glances that held both amusement and a touch of genuine concern. One of the other boys murmured, "If she gets hurt, Jacques will be very angry, Roland."

"Paul, you worry too much," the first boy answered. "We'll be easy on the *jeune fille*, won't we?"

Some of the other boys laughed. Cindy, gritting her teeth, vowed that she'd show these macho morons that American girls were made of sterner stuff. She sat down on one of the benches and accepted the loan of a helmet, elbow pads, and shin guards, positioning the safety equipment, then pulling on the thick sweater she had brought along to cover her T-shirt. The air above the ice was cool. When she had laced up her skates, Roland came over and offered her a hand.

"Come on, *américaine,* I'll give you a few pointers."

"My name is Cindy," the middle Lewis told him in a dignified tone. To her private satisfaction, she rose easily without his aid.

Roland grinned and nodded. "*Voilà,* Cindy. Here is a *bâton*—a hockey stick to you, and this is a *rondelle,* a puck. We hit the *rondelle* with the *bâton* into the *filet,* the net, to score."

Cindy, ignoring his condescending tone with some difficulty, nodded.

"There are a few other rules, of course," the dark-haired boy went on, grinning. "But this is enough to start, I think. Shall we take a few passes down the ice?"

"Ready when you are," Cindy told him. She skated smoothly toward the center of the ice, holding her stick and watching for his next move.

Roland skimmed across the ice with the ease of long practice, propelling the small puck with first one side of his stick, then the other, with graceful efficiency.

Cindy, skating quickly to catch up with him, reached with her stick to try to take away the puck.

But Roland skipped the small flat puck across the ice to another team member, and Cindy, over-extended, lost her balance and fell forward onto the cold ice, scraping her face painfully.

She bit back a groan. No way would she show pain in front of these guys; they'd probably expect her to burst into tears. *Jeune fille,* indeed!

"Are you hurt?" one of the boys asked.

Cindy shook her head stubbornly, though her cheek burned, while she scrambled to her feet.

"Let's try that again," she said grimly.

Roland took control of the puck and again Cindy raced after him, sure that this time she would scoop the puck away. But as the boy slid effortlessly ahead on his skates, and Cindy moved in for the kill, she suddenly discovered that Roland had left the puck behind to be scooped up by another teammate. Cindy, too far ahead to fight for it, could only stare.

"Good drop pass, Roland," one of the other boys called.

Cindy gritted her teeth.

On the next attempt, she almost succeeded in stealing the puck, but just as she reached the end of the rink, the boys around her reversed themselves effortlessly, and skated backwards. Cindy, trying to imitate their quick reversal, instead toppled straight backward, meeting the ice with painful force.

"Would you like to stop and take a rest?" Rolland asked her, while she awkwardly scrambled to her feet, resisting the urge to rub her sore bottom. He sounded genuinely concerned, but

Cindy, glancing up at him, caught just a glimpse of impish humor in his dark eyes.

"I'm fine," she declared flatly, determined to uphold the California spirit against these northern know-it-alls. "Let's go."

Roland shrugged, and the game continued.

Meanwhile, Nicole, turning the pages of her textbook, was feeling even more discouraged than her sister. She had left the Gilbert home early in order to have some time alone to study, but today the class was still as intimidating as it had been in the first session.

For years Nicole had been the star pupil of her French classes at Vista High. But all the students here were very proficient in French, and she had lost her unconscious edge. No longer achieving her laurels with little effort, for the first time Nicole began to appreciate what it must be like for the less-gifted students. Discouraged, it was hard for her to concentrate on the teacher's rapid discourse, or follow his lightning swift explanations. No longer confident that she would do well, she was beginning to worry that she would even pass!

Failing this class wouldn't imperil her college entrance; this class would only give her extra college credit. But the effect on her spirit could be disastrous. She had been ready to leave home and conquer the world. Now it appeared that the world was a more fearsome opponent than she had realized.

Overcome with depression, Nicole realized that her name had been called. Blushing, she looked to the front of the room.

"Mademoiselle Lewis?" The professor regarded her sternly.

Nicole had hardly heard the question, and she certainly had no idea what the answer was.

As everyone stared at her, she had to mutter, *"Je ne sais pas."* She didn't know the answer. Nicole Lewis had to admit total ignorance!

This completely unprecendented experience was also completely humiliating. She sank lower in her seat, wishing she could sink all the way through the floor.

The teacher looked stern, but he repeated the question.

Nicole, listening closely to his rapid French, discovered that he was asking the identity of the first French dramatist to apply the "three unities" to drama.

Nicole, relieved that she knew the answer— Corneille, of course, who took the unities of space, time, and action from Aristotle—responded.

The professor frowned and repeated her sentence, correcting the verb.

Nicole blushed again. She had used the wrong tense! What an elementary and embarrassing mistake. She stifled a groan and stared at her notebook, afraid to look around at the other students. They would think she was utterly stupid, completely unfit for this class.

What if she failed the course; how would she explain to her parents, who expected her to do well? Or to Madame Preston, her French teacher, who had gone to so much trouble to get her into this special class?

Nicole, who had never been a clock-watcher, stole a covert glance at her watch and prayed for this interminable class to end.

At the conclusion of class, the instructor handed out a sheet of essays the students had written the day before. Nicole, accustomed to good marks, held her breath. Perhaps this would make up for her mistakes in class.

But when she opened the front of the folder, her paper seemed to drip red ink!

"Oh, no," Nicole murmured. "My first bad grade!" When the class was dismissed, Nicole hurried for the door.

"Nicole?"

Nicole looked around to see Gabriella, the dark-haired girl she had met the first day, smiling at her.

"Would you like to get something cool to drink?"

"No, thanks." Nicole shook her head. "Another time, perhaps. I have a lot of work to do."

She would review her verb tenses, in addition to studying the next day's assignment. She didn't see the Canadian girl look after her, a puzzled expression on her face.

When Nicole got off the bus, walking slowly, impeded more by her lingering discouragement than the armload of books she carried, she saw the youngest Lewis at the end of the block, waving in recognition.

"Did you bring home the whole library?" Mollie asked, blinking at the size of Nicole's load.

"No." Nicole shook her head. "Just trying to get

a head start on tomorrow's lesson. I didn't exactly impress anybody today."

Mollie, startled to hear that Nicole, the model student, was having trouble with her class work, felt a rush of sympathy. "That's tough, Nicole. I thought I was the only Lewis who had to struggle with schoolwork."

Nicole's laugh held a bitter note, and Mollie stared at her sister, her concern growing. But then they both noticed another familiar figure coming down the street, and all thought of school problems was forgotten.

"Cindy!" Mollie cried. "Did you get mugged?"

Cindy, trying to grin despite her swollen lip and the scrape on her right cheek, shook her head. Limping, she caught up with her sisters.

"Just a little hockey practice," she explained, trying to walk briskly and not reveal just how bruised and sore she really felt.

"Mon dieu," Nicole gasped. "You didn't get into a fight, did you?"

"Of course not," Cindy answered, glaring at her sister. "I'm just trying to show these dumb jocks that Americans can play hockey as well as the local team!"

Mollie stared as Cindy stalked on ahead of her toward the Gilbert residence.

Nicole groaned. "By the time Cindy's through, she'll probably have started her own private war with Canada!"

Chapter 9

*M*ollie *woke the next morning to a cacoph-*
ony of groans. Alarmed, she sat up in bed and
saw Cindy trying to ease her battered body out
from beneath the covers.

"Cindy, what's wrong?"

Cindy, abashed to discover her usually somno-
lent little sister wide awake, immediately tried to
shrug off her soreness.

"Nothing, shrimp; go back to sleep."

"But you were making dreadful noises."

"You must have been dreaming," Cindy contradicted. "I'm going to take a hot bath."

Soaking in a tub of warm water eased some of
her stiff muscles, but Cindy, who was accustomed
to minor scrapes, still suffered from the blow to
her ego.

Hockey was not an easy sport to learn, that
was for sure! But giving up never occurred to her.

As stubborn as she was optimistic, Cindy never doubted that she'd get the knack of this intriguing new pastime. Besides, she had a thing or two to prove to these northern jocks!

At breakfast Nicole lingered long enough to give Cindy another lecture about diplomacy.

"If you tell me one more time that I'm representing my country in everything I do, I'm going to barf," Cindy told her angrily.

Nicole, shuddering, was only thankful that Madame Gilbert had gone back to the kitchen and didn't hear.

She glanced toward Mollie for help, but this time the youngest Lewis only grinned. "If you're looking for a diplomat, Cindy's not the right candidate. Besides, she's just as rude at home as she is abroad, Nicole."

Nicole, picking up her books, gave the middle Lewis a baleful glance. "Try to stay out of trouble, Cindy," she pleaded. Without much hope that her plea would be effective, but too worried about her own problems to waste any more time, she hurried away.

"Thanks a lot, shrimp," Cindy murmured to Mollie. "I think I like it better when you're not trying to take my side."

Mollie grinned and took another delicious croissant to dunk in her café au lait.

"You're going to grow out of all your clothes if you keep that up," Cindy warned, and Mollie wavered, one bite already in her mouth.

"I'll work it off with some extra exercise today," she pledged. "Maybe I'll come down and skate with you, Cindy. I can try to be nice enough to make up for your lack of couth."

"Ha! You just want to make eyes at all the guys," Cindy protested.

"All guys—really?" Mollie was interested at once.

"And you can't skate while hockey practice is going on; that's why the guys meet early, before regular rink hours."

Mollie's eyes were still bright with interest. "Then I'll just watch; I'll skate later. Maybe I can find someone who would like to give me some pointers— on the ice, I mean."

"I know what you mean," Cindy murmured into her orange juice. Once the idea had been planted, Mollie was not to be deterred. She went back upstairs, glad that she'd packed a few sweaters, and looked for the most becoming outfit to wear on the ice.

Cindy headed for the kitchen with the breakfast dishes and wondered how she could sneak out of the house without her little sister tagging along. When she had finished cleaning up, she slipped into the hall, picked up her duffle bag with her sweater and extra jeans—falling on the ice, she'd discovered, could get you very damp— and tip-toed toward the front door.

"Wait for me!" Mollie called from the stairway, and Cindy sighed. Caught.

They walked down to the bus stop together, and Mollie chattered all the way to the sports complex. When they got off the bus, Mollie finally stopped talking and followed her sister quietly toward the back of the building. She was a little startled to find Cindy walking nonchalantly into the locker room—true, no one was actually stripped down, but still—just like Cindy not to give the matter a second thought.

Mollie, throwing an aggrieved glance at her sister, murmured, "I'll be waiting in the stands," and made a rapid exit.

"Hey, Cindy," Roland yelled from across the room. "Who's the pretty *jeune fille?*"

"That's my sister; she's only fourteen, and whether or not she's pretty is a matter of opinion." Cindy, not meaning to sound ungracious, had more important things on her mind than adolescent mooning over Mollie. She was too busy rehearsing the moves she had thought out last night, hoping to make a better showing on the ice today than she had the day before.

Unfortunately, it was another day of spills and chills—Cindy, collecting more bruises than goals, became increasingly disgusted with herself. The worst part was that the Canadian boys played with disgusting fairness, so she couldn't even blame her poor performance on anyone else.

"The fact is, Lewis," she murmured to herself, as a melee of skates and sticks sent her sprawling across the ice and into the side of the rink, where she collided with a heavy-set boy, "you're pretty lousy at this game!"

The thought did not improve her temper. Snarling at the player she had just bumped into, Cindy pulled herself back to her feet and hurried to catch up with the fast-moving play.

Mollie watched quietly with real interest from

the stands. She had not accompanied Cindy and their dad to the Los Angeles Kings hockey matches and knew little about the game. It looked to her as if her headstrong sister was trying hard to get herself killed.

"Yikes, Cindy!" Mollie shrieked, watching Cindy go down yet again in a tangle of limbs and sticks.

One of the boys on the ice heard her and skated closer to give her a reassuring smile. "She's all right; she's—how do you say—a tough acorn, your sister."

Mollie giggled. "I think you mean tough nut, but thanks for the encouragement." She narrowed her eyes a bit to study the boy more closely; beneath the bulky pads of his uniform she could tell he was tall and slender; short, dark hair framed a long, thoughtful face. A nice face, Mollie thought.

His dark brown eyes seemed to smile back at her with particular warmth. Mollie, who had plenty of practice in picking up subtle hints from the male sex, brightened at his apparent interest.

"You're very good," she told him.

The tall boy grinned shyly. *"Merci beaucoup,"* he said gravely. "I have played hockey for years."

Then a shout from the other boys drew him away, and he skated rapidly back across the rink. Mollie watched him go, almost forgetting her concern over Cindy.

It was true, she thought. He did skate with special grace, and out of all the accomplished players, this boy stood out, even to Mollie's unpracticed eyes. But it was more than his skill that made her keep her gaze fastened on him; it was the gentle kindness that had prompted him to reassure a worried stranger as well as the shy interest Mollie was sure she had detected during their brief conversation. She wished she had asked his name. She listened closely as the boys shouted to one another, hoping to hear someone call it out.

"Paul," Mollie murmured to herself. "I like it."

When the team called a break, several of the players drifted over to the side to get a closer look at the petite, pretty Californian who didn't seem to be as belligerent as her more athletic sister.

Mollie, delighted, smiled demurely at them all, sure that Paul would join the group, and pleased to be the center of attention. *"Bonjour,"* she said, eager to try out her scant French vocabulary. *"Je m'appelle* Mollie."

"Comment ça va, Mollie?" one of the boys, short but with wide shoulders and dancing blue eyes, answered. *"Je m'appelle Raoul."*

"I'm fine, I mean, *très bien,"* Mollie answered, beginning to worry as she searched her memory for more conversation. "Do you speak English at all?"

This drew a shout of laughter. *"Mais oui,"* Raoul assured her. "We study it in school, you see."

"Good," Mollie said, sighing with relief. "My French isn't exactly perfect."

"You can say that again," Cindy observed. "You wouldn't believe what she came up with the other day at the café—"

"Cindy, don't you dare repeat that!" Mollie

shrieked, forgetting to be dignified in her alarm.
That anecdote was not one Mollie wanted floating
around this group of good-looking young men!

Cindy grinned, rubbing her sore shoulder. "Relax, shrimp." She flexed her sore muscles while
the rest of the boys continued to congregate
around her little sister. What morons they were!

"Then you can practice your French, and we
will help you, yes?" Raoul suggested.

Mollie nodded. "Why were you yelling about a
bird?" she asked.

"A bird?" Raoul looked blank.

"You said, *'hirondelle.'* Isn't that a kind of bird?"

Another shout of laughter rose from the group.

"It's *rondelle* we were saying, *jolie* Mollie," Raoul
explained. "The hockey puck—that is what we
are chasing—not a bird!"

Mollie, grinning good-naturedly at her mistake,
couldn't resist a quick peek toward Paul. But he
was at the outer fringe of the group, seemingly
content to allow someone else to capture her
attention as he examined a loose binding on one
of his shin pads. Mollie felt absurdly disappointed.
Had she been mistaken after all? Wasn't he interested in her?

Then he raised his head, and their eyes met. For
a moment Mollie was sure that his glance was
warm and eager, and she smiled. But Paul looked
away again, and she felt more confused than ever.

She brought her attention hurriedly back to
Raoul, who was still speaking. "After the rink
opens, you are going to skate?"

"I thought I would," Mollie answered. "I'm not very good, though."

There was a chorus of eager volunteers as several boys hastened to assure Mollie that expert tutelage was readily available. Cindy, listening to the conversation as she tried to rub out yet another bruise, couldn't keep from grinning. This should make Mollie's day—a whole team of good-looking guys to choose from.

When she glanced up she saw that although Mollie accepted the boys' offers graciously, her smile seemed a little forced. The youngest Lewis seemed happy, but not ecstatic.

Cindy wrinkled her nose. Had she missed something?

Chapter 10

*M*ollie stayed until the hockey practice ended and the rink opened to the public, then skated, with ample opportunity to flirt with several of the team members—just about any of them, in fact, except the one boy she kept hoping would seek her out. But he didn't.

She went home in a very silent mood. Cindy, if she'd had the energy to notice, would have been puzzled indeed. But she went off to soak in another tub of hot water, trying to relax her strained muscles.

Mollie, coming into the bathroom to look for her hairbrush, frowned at her sister, almost hidden in the large, old-fashioned tub. "You're as black and blue as a jaybird, Cindy. Don't you think you should switch to a less risky sport?"

"Nope," Cindy told her firmly. "I'm going to learn how to play hockey or die trying."

"I'll send flowers," Mollie warned, her tone dark.

When Cindy finally pulled herself out of the cooling water and dressed, she was surprised to find Mollie curled up on the bed, staring at the green-leaved trees that swayed outside the windowsill.

"What's with you?"

But her sister didn't seem to hear. Frowning, Cindy shut the wardrobe door rather noisily. Still Mollie didn't look around. Finally Cindy walked over and touched her sister's shoulder.

Mollie jumped. "Don't sneak up on me like that!"

Cindy, perplexed, stared at her sister. "I didn't exactly sneak up on you," she told her. "You were a million miles away. Is something wrong?"

"No." Mollie shook her head, but she didn't quite meet her sister's glance.

"Want to walk down to the park?"

Mollie shook her head again. "I don't think so; you go ahead."

"Expecting a call from one of the team?" Cindy made an educated guess, but to her surprise, Mollie looked positively doleful.

"No," she said again.

Cindy gave up. "I'll see you at dinner," she told her sister, who nodded, but already seemed lost in her own dream world.

After several hours in the park, Cindy headed back toward the Gilbert residence. At the end of the block, she saw Nicole getting off the bus and lengthened her stride to catch up with her sister.

"How was class?"

Nicole looked morose. "Don't ask."

"Not you, too!" Cindy's answer was oblique, but Nicole didn't even notice. "Want to go to a movie tonight?"

Nicole shook her head. "I've got too much studying to do."

Cindy opened the gate and allowed her older sister to precede her up the path. "Real lively bunch," she murmured to herself. But Nicole didn't seem to hear.

To Cindy's surprise, the normally late-rising Mollie got up early and accompanied her sister to hockey practice for the rest of the week. Mollie continued to attract considerable attention from the male members of the team, but to Cindy's mystification, she didn't even seem delighted. She sure wasn't acting like the boy-crazy Mollie Cindy was used to, but Cindy couldn't figure out what was wrong. She didn't know that the one boy Mollie most wanted to attract remained as elusive as ever.

Mollie couldn't understand it. Just when she had told herself for the tenth time that she would forget about Paul and enjoy the attentions of the other boys, she would catch him looking her way with an expression of such wistful eagerness that her hopes would rise once more. But each time the players took a break, and the other boys crowded around Mollie, Paul continued to hang back.

Mollie didn't know what to do. "Forget about

him," she told herself, trying to listen to Raoul's latest story, or Antoine's newest joke.

But when the boys returned to their practice, Mollie couldn't help picking out Paul's tall form as he moved swiftly over the ice, or help noticing his automatic sportsmanship when another player fell and Paul was the first to help him to his feet.

What was a girl to do?

One Friday afternoon, Cindy glanced through the pile of messages beside the phone, looking in vain for her own name. All she could find were messages for her little sister.

"Message for Mollie from Raoul: 'would you like to go skating?' Message for Mollie from Antoine: invitation to the theater. Another call from Raoul. Mollie needs a social secretary!"

Yet when Cindy climbed the stairs, expecting to find Mollie dressed for a date, she found her sister in jeans and an old sweatshirt, looking unusually unkempt for the always-meticulous Lewis.

"Aren't you going out tonight?" Cindy asked in surprise.

Mollie shook her head.

"But what about all those phone calls? Were you out with someone else this afternoon?" Cindy, wondering what kind of pickle Mollie had gotten herself into this time, narrowed her eyes.

But Mollie only shrugged. "I was in the garden helping Madame Gilbert weed the flower beds."

"But didn't you call back any of those boys?"

Mollie shook her head.

"Why not?" Cindy was becoming genuinely concerned at this un-Mollie-like behavior, and she began to wonder if she should ask Madame Gilbert to take Mollie's temperature.

Mollie shook her head. "I decided to stay home tonight."

Cindy wrinkled her brow. Something was *definitely* wrong. But she had to wait until after the evening meal before she found a chance to talk to Nicole alone.

"Something's wrong with Mollie," she said bluntly.

Nicole, lost in thought as usual, looked up sharply. "What are you talking about?"

'I don't know what it is, but something's wrong," Cindy insisted stubbornly. "She's been moping around all week, and she hardly touched her food tonight. Didn't you notice?"

Cindy, unable to resist the small jab, felt a stirring of satisfaction as Nicole, for the first time in days, appeared to focus on her sister's words.

"I didn't—I mean, I thought Mollie was having fun. Do you know what's wrong?"

Cindy shook her head. "She hasn't confided in me; *you're* the one she usually talks to, at least, you were until you decided to forget our existence."

Nicole flushed, and Cindy almost regretted her remark. But it was true. Nicole had hardly spoken to either of them since their arrival in Quebec City. Cindy, accustomed to an easy rapport with her older sister, felt abandoned. She knew that Nicole was growing up, but she hadn't expected such an abrupt chasm to open between them. Too proud to admit her own sense of loss, Cindy didn't mind pointing out that Nicole was also neglecting the baby of the family.

Nicole's smooth forehead wrinkled as she grimaced, her blue eyes shadowed with guilt. "I didn't think—maybe she's homesick, Cindy. Mollie's never stayed away from home for more than a few days before."

Cindy shrugged.

"I'll take her out tomorrow," Nicole promised, smothering a sigh as she remembered the essay she should be working on this weekend. But Mollie was her sister; Nicole had to consider her sibling's welfare.

If Mollie had stayed at home, I wouldn't have had to worry about her. Nicole pushed back the half-guilty, half-angry thought. "I'll spend Saturday with her," she promised more firmly, and her conscience quieted.

The next morning, determined to make up for her neglect, Nicole harried Mollie into an early start. Since Cindy was out jogging, and there was no hockey practice scheduled, Mollie grudgingly agreed. They headed for the lower town, by way of the *l'escalier Casse-Cou*, or Breakneck Stairway.

As they made their way down the winding, crowded passage, Nicole pointed out tiny, attractive boutiques on the different levels, but Mollie only nodded, showing no inclination to stop and look for bargains. Nicole's sense of concern grew.

They walked on to the *Maison Chevalier*, an impressive group of gray-stone buildings, built as three houses in 1699 and later joined into one massive residence. The girls wandered through the museum, admiring the wood beams and polished wooden floors, stone fireplaces, and antique furnishings.

Mollie, aware of Nicole's effort, tried her best to look interested in pewter place settings and four-poster beds, and giggled over a double chair in one of the bedrooms, just right for "Mama and Papa." But whenever she thought Nicole wasn't looking, Mollie's thoughts tended to wander, and once she caught Nicole regarding her with a serious expression.

"Mollie," Nicole hesitated. "Would you like to go home early? You don't have to stay in Quebec for the whole length of the class just because I do, you know."

To her dismay, Mollie's blue eyes filled with tears. "I don't want to go home," she blurted, and hurried ahead of her sister while she fought to control herself.

Nicole felt more confused than ever.

Later, when they had returned home, Nicole left Mollie to climb the staircase and made her way through the hall and out the garden door to look for Cindy.

She found the middle Lewis curled up in a wicker chair, listening to her Walkman and enjoying—though she would never have admitted it— her respite from the grueling hockey practice.

Nicole gestured to Cindy to remove her earphones.

"I don't know what's wrong with Mollie," she

said without preamble. "But she isn't acting like herself at all."

"That's what I thought," Cindy nodded. "Did you ask if something was bothering her?"

"I told her she could go home early if she wanted to," Nicole said. "But she got upset, Cindy. She won't talk to me."

"Can you blame her?" Cindy's tone was dry. "You've been pretty wrapped up in your own concerns since we got here, Nicole."

Nicole frowned. "I've had a lot on my mind," she muttered.

Cindy's green eyes narrowed. "We know you're getting ready to leave the nest, Nicole, but it's tough on us fledglings being left behind."

"Give me a break, Cindy."

"Yeah." Cindy got up from her comfortable chair and headed inside, deciding to take a stab at Mollie herself.

She found the youngest Lewis lying across one of the white comforters, her face almost hidden beneath a lace-covered pillow. Cindy suspected that the other girl had been crying.

"Hey," she said, her normally gruff tone softened by concern. "What's with you, anyhow?"

"I don't know what you mean." Mollie's voice, if a bit shaky, was unusually dignified.

Cindy sat down beside her sister, impressed despite herself.

"What's up, shrimp? You're not going out, you don't want to shop or dress up or eat; this isn't normal!"

Mollie looked mutinous. "Can't a girl have any privacy around here?"

"Not when she has two sisters," Cindy answered matter-of-factly. "Well, I'm not sure Nicole counts anymore. But I still notice. Are you homesick?"

"No." Mollie shook her head, but her blue eyes flooded with tears, and she struggled to hold them back.

"Then what is it?"

Mollie swallowed, then spoke softly. "You won't laugh?"

"Promise."

"Paul doesn't like me." The dark secret out, Mollie's tears flowed unheeded.

Cindy stared. "Paul? Paul who?"

Mollie looked indignant. "Paul Denière, you know, on the hockey team."

"Oh," Cindy observed, still looking blank. "That tall boy who's so quiet—the one with the terrific wrist shots?"

"I guess," Mollie, no hockey connoisseur, responded.

"But Mollie," Cindy went on, trying to decipher this puzzle. "He's hardly spoken to you."

"I know. That's the trouble," Mollie wailed.

"But what about all the other—"

"I don't *care* about anyone else," Mollie said with exasperation.

Cindy blinked. This was a new Mollie, and Cindy hardly knew what to say.

"You're serious, aren't you, shrimp?" she finally commented, not unkindly.

Mollie nodded. "He doesn't like me," she whispered, overcome with grief.

Cindy, ever practical, shrugged her shoulders. "How can you be so sure? Sitting here and pining away isn't going to make him notice you, Mollie. Go out with some of the other boys—plenty of them are willing. Then maybe Paul will take notice."

"You think so?"

"It beats sitting here and feeling sorry for yourself," Cindy told her bluntly.

But Mollie didn't take offense. "I guess it's worth a try," she agreed glumly.

Chapter 11

*D*riven by desperation, Mollie lost no time putting Cindy's plan into action. On Monday she accompanied Cindy to hockey practice as usual, and this time the youngest Lewis didn't discourage the other boys who flocked around her during their breaks.

Raoul, who was compact and sturdy, with broad shoulders and straight dark brows, was delighted to find the elusive *jolie* Mollie ready to smile at his pleasantries.

"Perhaps you would like to have lunch with me after practice," he asked. "Then we could take a walk; I will show you more of our *belle ville.*"

To his obvious delight, Mollie smiled sweetly. "Quebec *is* a beautiful city," she agreed. "And I'd love to see more of it with you."

Raoul rejoined the game in great spirits; Mollie watched hopefully as he exchanged a few words with Paul Denière. Paul glanced her way, and Mollie waited for some sign of jealousy or incipient competition. Much to her chagrin, he only shrugged and smiled.

Mollie sank back down onto the bleachers, her hopes dashed once more. "It isn't working," she murmured to herself. "What am I going to do?"

But she had committed herself, so Mollie left with Raoul after practice, trying to look happy and fighting the urge to look back over her shoulder for one last glimpse of Paul.

They had lunch at a sidewalk café, and then Raoul led the way to the Battlefields Park.

"Voilà, Mollie," Raoul told her, grinning. "This is a monument to the British general, Wolf."

Mollie, who had already visited the monument with Nicole, didn't have the heart to tell him, so she just smiled and nodded. "Very nice."

If the Canadian boy noticed that the girl who had been so animated and cheerful at the ice rink had become very quiet and subdued, he apparently put it down to a sudden attack of shyness, and tried even harder to amuse her. They walked down to the old Quebec Jail, and Raoul told her stories about the *Petit Bastille.*

"The Bastille was a famous old prison in Paris, wasn't it?" Mollie asked, brushing a wisp of blond hair out of her eyes.

"Mais oui," Raoul nodded. "Haven't you read about it in history?"

Mollie, who had remembered the famous building from an old movie, blushed.

They walked through the park, admiring the

colorful flowers in neatly kept beds, finally stopping before another statue, this time of Joan of Arc.

"She was pretty," Mollie noted, gazing up at the famous saint on horseback.

"Not as pretty as you," Raoul told her. He tried to take her hand, but Mollie slipped away, unable to go on with this insincere flirtation.

"Would you like to ride in a *calèche?*" Raoul offered generously. "It would be fun, Mollie."

Mollie, who had been longing to ride in one of the horse-drawn carriages ever since she had arrived in Quebec, shook her head. In her daydream, there was another boy sitting beside her; another boy holding her hand. This just wouldn't do.

And it wasn't fair to Raoul, she suddenly realized, to spend time with him just to interest another boy. Was this what love did to you? Mollie felt older, and almost motherly as she gazed at Raoul's eager expression. He was a nice boy. She really felt sorry that he wasn't the one she felt this inexplicable attraction for.

"Raoul," Mollie said, her sympathy making her tone kinder than she realized, "I'm afraid I have to go home now."

"Perhaps tomorrow we will go out again, yes?" Raoul suggested.

"Maybe," Mollie hedged.

They walked back to Madame Gilbert's residence, and Raoul said a decorous good-bye at the gate, not—to Mollie's relief—attempting a good-bye kiss.

She waved and turned up the front path, feeling guilty. Raoul was too nice to use like this, but how else was she going to attract Paul's attention?

No one else was at home. Madame Gilbert had mentioned at breakfast that she had shopping to do, Nicole was still at school, and Cindy—who knows?—was probably still on the ice trying to refine her skating technique.

Mollie wandered out to the sunny back garden and curled up in a comfortable wicker chair. For a long time she sat in the soft afternoon sunlight, lost in thought. Then a sound from the wall made her look up. The neighbor's cat was staring at her inquiringly.

"Hello, kitty," Mollie encouraged.

The cat meowed softly and dropped lightly off the top of the fence, padding its way over to Mollie's chair and allowing itself to be petted.

Mollie, suddenly missing her own animals at home, swallowed hard against the lump in her throat. A treacherous tear slipped out of the corner of her eye and dropped down onto the yellow fur.

"Mollie," someone said from behind her.

Mollie looked over her shoulder to see Nicole staring at her, looking worried.

"Mollie, are you sure you wouldn't like to go home early?"

Mollie burst into tears and, while the startled cat jumped hastily out of her path, ran for the house.

"You don't understand anything!" she yelled.

Nicole stared after her younger sister, frowning in bewilderment.

* * *

The next morning, Cindy was astounded to find Mollie up before her.

"Is something wrong?" she demanded.

"What do you mean?" Mollie refused to look at her as she drew a brush through her long wavy hair.

"You never get up this early," Cindy said. "I know the guys at the rink are nuts over you, but even so—"

"Oh, shut up." Mollie, irritated beyond bearing by this sisterly blindness, threw down her hairbrush and stormed out the door.

Cindy blinked, her expression a combination of dismay and bewilderment.

"Nicole," she said, "What are we going to do? There's definitely something wrong with Mollie and this is even worse than that time we went camping and she pretended to be so independent."

Nicole looked up from her books. "I know. I don't know what to do about her."

Cindy shrugged, unable to think of a solution herself. She said, "Well, she'll come out of it sooner or later. Come on, I smell something good in the kitchen."

At breakfast the three girls were carefully polite to each other and to Madame Gilbert, but no one really cared to talk. Nicole, as usual, was worrying about her class, hoping that today she would be able to answer the professor correctly. Cindy, whose collection of bruises made her trim, tanned body resemble an abstract painting, wondered if she would ever attain any kind of skill as a hockey player, and Mollie could think only of Paul—so near and yet so unobtainable.

Nicole soon left to catch her bus, and Cindy and Mollie cleared away the breakfast dishes and were out of the house in half an hour. Cindy glanced a couple of times at her little sister, but Mollie, still brooding, didn't notice.

The boys greeted Mollie enthusiastically, and she tried to smile in response, but it was becoming harder and harder to pretend. While Cindy put on her gear, Raoul hurried over to speak to the youngest Lewis.

Mollie, feeling guilty again at the sight of his broad smile, decided that she couldn't go out with the hockey player again. It would be different if she thought that she might really like Raoul, but nice as he was, there was simply no one else she wanted to spend time with, not with Paul Denière's face engraved on her mind's eye. When Raoul smiled and said, "Would you like to go for a walk this afternoon, Mollie? Or perhaps take that ride in the *calèche*—it's a very nice day."

Mollie shook her head and tried to make her tone firm. "No, Raoul, I'm sorry."

The boy looked downcast. Another player, redhaired Antoine, whose mischievous grin would normally have attracted Mollie right away, winked at the California teenager.

"You're right, Mollie. Raoul is too—how do you say—boring! Now, me, I could show you how to have the good time."

Raoul turned on his teammate, his normally good-natured expression turning dark. "Boring!" He stalked forward, his stocky body tense.

But Antoine continued to laugh. "You, you are the original bore, Raoul."

Raoul lifted one hand menacingly, and Mollie, her eyes wide, drew a deep breath. "Stop it, both of you. I don't want to go out with either one of you—so there!"

Both boys, startled by this impulsive outburst, stared at Mollie in surprise, then looking a little sheepish, turned back to the rink and pretended to be very busy adjusting their safety gear.

Cindy, who had heard this minidrama, raised her eyebrows as she fastened her skates. "What is going on around here?" she murmured to herself.

Mollie, withdrawing to the outer edge of the stand, sat down and watched the rest of the practice in solitary peace, certain only that if she didn't have Paul's affection, she didn't care about anyone else's.

Meanwhile, Cindy, who had finally been given a chance to play center, was diving after the elusive hockey puck. Starting from the middle of the forward line, she led the rush toward the opposite goal, trying her best to keep control of the puck. She tried for a shot at the goal but found her path blocked by two defensemen skating backwards. She hesitated, knowing that she should pass the puck to one of the wings, who were in a better position to score. But Cindy, who hadn't yet scored in all the practice games she and the boys had played, longed to get one point on her own. As she drew back to try a slap shot, one of the opposing players zoomed in and snatched away the puck.

She rushed to save it, but instead rocketed into another player and plummeted to the ice.

She heard Raoul call, "Good shot," and looked up to see who had made the score. Roland, of course.

"Are you all right, Cindy?" one of the boys asked when she made no move to sit up.

"Sure," Cindy groaned. "This is my natural position, haven't you noticed?" Amid scattered laughter, she sighed and pushed herself up to a sitting position, rubbing her cheek to drive away the chill of the icy rink.

"You don't give up, do you, Cindy," Roland remarked, his tone one of grudging respect.

Cindy grinned and shook her head. "Nope. But I don't think I'm going to turn into a great hockey player in the next few weeks."

A shout of laughter greeted her candid admission.

"Cindy," Antoine began, grinning himself. "We've been playing hockey for years, since we were Pee-Wees."

"What's that?" Cindy asked.

"You know—the hockey teams organized for children," Paul explained patiently.

"Oh, something like our Little League," Cindy said, nodding in understanding. "Well, it shows. I hate to admit it, but you guys are really the best."

The boys gathered around her, laughing again. "*Merci*, Cindy," Roland said. "I will tell you something, too; when you started, I only wanted to show you how we played because I thought you had—how do you say—the big mouth."

Cindy grinned. "Right on one."

Roland chuckled. "But now that you have played with us, I will tell you. For a beginner, Cindy Lewis, you have done very well."

"More than well," Antoine agreed, while the other boys nodded.

Cindy felt a rush of pleasure as her last scrap of resentment faded. "Thanks, guys. I've really enjoyed it, despite all the bruises." She rubbed her elbow as she spoke.

Then the irrepressible Roland added, "If you continue practicing, in time you could be a first-rate player, Cindy. For a girl, that is."

"What?" Cindy, her ready temper flaring, glared up at him.

Roland winked, while the rest of the team laughed at her momentary outburst.

"You're hopeless." Cindy shook her head at the unrepentant Roland. "Come on, let's get this game back in play!"

With lots of hands ready to offer a friendly assist, Cindy got to her feet and the boys skated off to their positions. She had a huge grin on her face as she waited for the play to begin. She had forgotten all about the scrape on her cheek, her sore arm, and her soaked jeans. Her grip on the hockey stick was firm but sure, she possessed a new-found confidence in her playing, and the team had finally accepted her as one of their own. This was heaven!

Cindy never thought to glance up at Mollie, who was sitting quietly in the very back of the stands. If she had looked, she would have seen a very sad Mollie, cheeks damp with tears and a gloomy expression that seemed to say the world was about to come to an end.

Across town, Nicole pored over her books. Although it was a beautiful day, bright and sunny with all the summer flowers in full bloom, and despite the fact that she'd made an adequate showing in class today, her mood was dark.

The fact was, Nicole was not accustomed to simply being adequate. "Face it, *idiot,*" she murmured to herself. "You've been a big frog in a small pond for too long."

Yet that sensible thought didn't lift her depression. What had happened to her glorious Canadian adventure? While Cindy was busy knocking herself black and blue, trying her best to break a bone, and Mollie was moping and wouldn't tell anyone why, here was Nicole just barely scraping through her class. She sighed, trying to concentrate on her textbook.

If she were home, she could sit down with a cup of coffee and tell her mother how discouraged she was. Nicole sighed again as she realized she had made a dreadful discovery; Mollie might not be homesick, but Nicole Lewis, almost eighteen, definitely was. How embarrassing!

One dire thought led to another. Next week was Nicole's eighteenth birthday! Busy with classwork, the important date had almost slipped her mind.

She had to swallow hard. She had waited so long for this birthday. She hadn't expected to spend it away from home, without her parents or friends to help her celebrate. At home in Santa Barbara, the Lewis family would have had a big celebration, with a special dinner featuring all Nicole's favorite foods, ending with an elaborate cake whipped up by her talented mother. Mr. Lewis would have opened a bottle of champagne and made a special toast, and all the girls would have been allowed a tiny glass, in honor of this special occasion. But she wasn't at home, and even her sisters seemed to have forgotten.

Nicole turned a page in her book and again tried to concentrate on her lesson. No need to be so dismal; at least she was doing a little better in class and the other students were slowly becoming more friendly, willing to accept her. But she still missed her parents and her old friends in Santa Barbara. Nicole was certainly too old to cry over a missed birthday dinner! But the lines on the page in front of her blurred in a distinctly suspicious manner.

Chapter 12

*M*ollie *got up early Friday, and as she had* done all week, prepared to go to the skating rink. But this time, deciding to avoid any more embarrassing encounters with Raoul and Antoine, she allowed Cindy to leave without her. Mollie left the house shortly afterward, catching the next bus and walking the rest of the now familiar route to the sporting complex.

When she slipped quietly in through the back entrance, the locker room was deserted, and she could hear sounds from the ice indicating the practice game was already underway.

She made her way into the rink area and chose a spot at the side of the stands that would allow her to watch the game, but not make her presence obvious. While the players skated madly from one side of the rink to the other, Mollie sat

in the shadows and watched for the one player
she could always distinguish from all the rest.

Paul. She had already memorized the slight
wave of brown hair that hung over his forehead,
the straight, strong set of his shoulders, his own
particular grace as he skated with such ease and
confidence over the ice. She loved to watch him
move so easily into the melee that was the hockey
game, and very often emerge from the pack with
the puck within his control.

Yet the fact that he was an outstanding player
was really irrelevant. Mollie knew she wouldn't
have cared if Paul had been the worst player on
the team. She would still have noted his courtesy
and cheerful good will toward the other players;
his good sportsmanship made her even prouder
of him than a skillful shot did. And the small
smile that lit up his rather solemn expression
whenever he scored a goal made Mollie's heart
turn flip-flops inside her chest.

It hurt that he wasn't interested in her, had
made no move to further their slight acquain-
tance. But he was still the only player on the ice
to Mollie's eyes. She hardly noticed how much
her sister was improving, or the fact that she
didn't land on the ice quite as often as she had
during her first week of practice.

The vigorous sport was still full of opportunities for mishaps, though. After an hour of play,
the first major accident of the day occurred. Mollie, watching closely, saw three skaters collide as
all dove for the puck. She heard the sound of

involuntary grunts, then the scrape of metal skates colliding. Without even knowing it, Mollie jumped up. Paul Denière was one of the players in the heap!

Two of the team got slowly to their feet, assisted by the other players, but Paul was not one of them. Mollie, her heart beating fast, saw that Paul still lay supine on the ice while several of the other players crowded around him, looking anxious.

He was hurt! Mollie forgot caution, forgot that she hadn't meant to be seen. She jumped down from the stands and ran toward the side of the rink as the boys helped Paul off the ice. Leaning heavily on Antoine's arm, Paul reached the bench at the side of the arena just as Mollie appeared.

"Oh, Paul," she cried, "are you all right?"

The tall boy looked up in surprise, the furrow of pain that creased his forehead easing as he was able to take his weight off his injured ankle.

"It's nothing," he told the concerned girl, sounding diffident. "Just a twisted ankle; I don't think it's sprained."

"They shouldn't have fallen on top of you—those monsters!" Mollie raged.

Paul blinked at this unexpected accusation, and Antoine grinned.

"Mollie, it was not a plot; do not call us *bêtes.*"

"You *are* beasts, if you hurt Paul," Mollie stormed, and the group at the edge of the ice stared at her in surprise. Mollie, unaware that her secret was out, glared back at them.

"You should have been more careful!"

Beneath her angry gaze, the other boys drew back a little, but continued to watch Paul and Mollie curiously.

"Ah, now I see why *jolie* Mollie would not walk with you," Antoine said to Raoul. "It is Paul who is the lucky one!"

Mollie, hearing the comment, blushed, her anger fading as she realized that she had exposed her secret attachment. She was afraid to look at Paul, afraid that he would look alarmed or even disgusted.

But, while she hesitated, Paul spoke softly. "I'm all right, Mollie. Thank you."

"I didn't mean—" Mollie began, miserably certain that she had lost any remaining chance with him by revealing her hidden feelings. "I mean, I'm sorry if—"

She faltered, aware of the other boys only a short distance away. She flushed, then tried again. "I didn't mean to make a spectacle of us both; I'm sorry."

Paul answered her quickly. "You have not made a spectacle, Mollie. I'm glad that you care if I'm hurt."

"You are?" Mollie took a deep breath. She was so overwhelmed by this unexpected revelation that she forgot they had an audience and blurted out, "But—I didn't think you liked me!"

Paul looked startled. "*Mais non,* how could I not like someone as sweet and *jolie* as you? But you had so many to pick from"—he nodded toward the other players—"I did not think that you could be interested in me, Mollie."

"Oh, but I don't care about them!" Mollie whispered earnestly.

But her rapt attention to Paul had already revealed more to the other boys than Mollie realized.

"We are dust beneath her feet," Antoine murmured, looking more amused than rejected.

Raoul gave a philosophical and very Gallic shrug. *"C'est la vie,"* he said.

"No, I think it's *l'amour,"* Antoine corrected, winking toward the two at the side of the rink.

Mollie, who had eyes only for Paul, didn't notice the other boys' comments.

"Do you really—do you think you could—do you like me, Paul?" she stammered, then turned even redder.

Paul didn't seem to mind her bluntness. *"Mais oui,* Mollie," he assured her.

Mollie sighed, almost light-headed with joy. "I'm so glad," she said simply. They smiled at each other.

Cindy, who had come to the edge of the rink to check on her injured comrade, looked puzzled. "Is Paul all right?"

"I think so," Antoine said.

"Well, isn't he coming back into the game?" All of a sudden Cindy noticed that Mollie's big blue eyes shone with happiness, and that Paul was staring into them with incredible fascination. She felt a growing sense of irritation when she realized they might be about to lose their best player just when she had begun to master the game. "Did he sprain his ankle or something?"

"No, just his heart," Antoine explained.

Cindy snorted and turned back toward the center of the rink. Everyone followed except Paul, who continued to stare at Mollie.

"I guess I should let you get back to the game," Mollie said, suddenly bashful.

Paul nodded, and stood up, testing his sore ankle. But he didn't seem in a hurry to leave.

"You're sure you're all right?"

Paul smiled at her concern, and Mollie, her heart beating faster, saw how his shy, slow smile lit up his dark eyes.

"I'm very well, thank you," he told her gravely. "Perhaps, after the game, you would like a cup of *café au lait?* If you have no plans already, I mean?"

Mollie glowed over this awkward invitation, more valuable to her than the most practiced flirtation from someone else.

"I'd love to," she assured him earnestly.

"Good," Paul said. "Let's go."

"Now?" Mollie glanced uncertainly toward the ice. "But the game's not over."

"It is for me," he told her seriously. "I will take off my gear. Meet me outside?"

"Absolutely," Mollie promised, giddy with happiness. She could have danced, floated across the floor. She found it very difficult to keep from skipping out the back exit.

From across the ice, Cindy groaned. "What on earth is he doing?" she said. "The game's not over."

Antoine and Raoul exchanged resigned glances. "Game called because of *mal d'amour*," Antoine suggested.

"What does that mean?" The middle Lewis looked perplexed.

"Sick with love," Roland explained.

"Trust Mollie to steal our best player," Cindy groaned.

Chapter 13

*M*ollie *would remember that day for the rest* of her life.

When Paul came out of the rear exit, he found Mollie waiting patiently.

"Shall we go to a café?" he asked, still looking a little uncertain.

"Oh, yes." Mollie, who would have eaten bread and water and counted it a feast in Paul's company, quickly reassured him.

He nodded, and they walked slowly toward the center of town. Paul, who had left his hockey gear in his locker, seemed not quite sure what to do with his hands. He finally thrust them into the pockets of his jeans.

Mollie, watching him from the corner of her eye, also felt shy. She had always been able to talk easily to boys, flirting with more assurance than most of her friends. Now, when she needed it, all her self-assurance seemed to have vanished.

When the silence seemed to stretch on too long, she finally pulled herself together and said, "Tell me about you."

Paul, who might also have been searching for something to say, gave her a quick glance.

"What do you want to know?"

His brown eyes were dark and warm as velvet, Mollie saw. With some difficulty, she remembered her question.

"Anything." She smiled up at him, and they both relaxed a little. "What grade are you in?"

"Grade?"

"In school, you know."

"Ah," he nodded. "I have just completed my fifth year in the *niveau secondaire*—secondary level."

"Oh." Mollie struggled to figure out what the equivalent would be at Vista.

Paul, seeing her bewilderment, tried to explain. "We have six years in the *niveau primaire,* or elementary school. Then we take an examination, and if we do well, go onto secondary."

"If you don't?" Mollie couldn't help asking.

"Then there is another year in elementary," he told her. "To make up."

"And the next year is your sixth year in secondary?" Mollie tried to sound as if she understood, but to her chagrin, he shook his head.

"*Mais non.* I have passed my examinations and received my *Certificant d'Etudes Secondaires.*"

"That sounds like a diploma." Mollie nodded wisely. "And then?"

"Next September I start at the CEGEP," he explained. *"College d'enseignement general et professionne."*

"No wonder they abbreviate it," Mollie giggled. "You're in college already? I didn't think you were that old."

"I'm sixteen; *et toi?*"

"Almost fifteen," Mollie assured him quickly. Then she realized that he had, consciously or otherwise, used the intimate form of the pronoun "you," and she had to glance away from his warm brown eyes.

"After four years of college, what do you want to be?"

"After two years at CEGEP, I hope to go to university." He grinned at her confusion, adding, "I hope my hockey will help me then—with a scholarship."

"You must be very smart." Mollie looked up at him again, admiration obvious in her eyes. Paul shrugged.

"I work hard, like everyone."

Mollie, her expression a comic mixture of guilt and eagerness, hastened to agree. "Of course."

He grinned and she had to add, "Well, sometimes I do."

Laughing, they crossed the avenue and Mollie discovered that they were already in the heart of the town. Taking the funicular to the Upper Town, they soon found a tiny table at a sidewalk café, and Mollie discovered that sitting with Paul was not at all like sharing a table with her sisters. A colorful umbrella shaded them from the sun; a steady stream of people strolled along the pavement, while a slight breeze stirred the warm air. Mollie, looking around, decided that this was truly romantic. No wonder Nicole had rhapsodized about French culture. Mollie privately decided she was definitely a convert.

They both ordered, and when the cups of thick, cream-topped café au lait arrived, sipped slowly. It was so perfect, Mollie almost feared that she would wake and find it all a dream.

"It's a beautiful day, *n'est-ce pas?*" she said to Paul. He nodded. Mollie felt as if the whole landscape glittered with special excitement, so potent was the magic of Paul's presence. "Quebec is *très belle*, she added, looking over the crowded avenue, the city's native population swelling with the summer tourist trade. She noticed that a cluster of ribbons and flowers now adorned the street corner, and she wondered if the whole city was celebrating her newfound love. Then, realizing that idea was rather unlikely, she turned to Paul and asked, "What are the decorations for?"

"The *Festival d'été* has begun," he told her. "The Summer Festival. It is great fun, Mollie, like one big party. I didn't get to share *la Saint-Jean* with you, Quebec's national day in June, when the clowns entertain in the streets, or the *Carnaval d'hiver*, the Winter Carnival, with our own *Bonhomme*, the big man of snow. But I can show you the Summer Festival, yes?"

"Oh, yes," Mollie agreed, breathless at the thought. Then she saw that his smile had widened. "What is it?"

"You have *une moustache*, Mollie."

Mollie gasped. "A mustache?" She reached the tip of her tongue up and tasted the thick cream that clung to the top of her lip. "Oh no!" She grabbed hastily for her napkin, while Paul chuckled.

"But a very *jolie moustache*," he teased.

Mollie, who saw that his smile was tender, smiled back at him. "I think I've had enough café," she said. "It's really too warm for a hot drink, anyhow. *Je suis chaude.*"

Mollie, who had only meant to say that she was feeling warm, saw Paul's smile deepen. He fought back another fit of laughter.

"What'd I say now?" Mollie demanded.

"You should say, *'J'ai chaud,'*" he corrected.

"Oh no, I did it again," Mollie said with a worried frown. "What did I say?"

"You said that you are—how do I say—looking for action." Paul's eyes twinkled.

Mollie felt her cheeks flush, and she covered her face with her hands. "Oh, no!"

"Do not be distressed, *ma petite*," Paul soothed. "I know what you meant to say; I understand."

Glancing up at his warm brown eyes and generous smile, Mollie saw that he did. She felt her embarrassment fade, and smiled back at him gratefully.

Leaving the café, they wandered through the streets, oblivious to their surroundings, holding hands and looking into each other's eyes.

Mollie, who had just learned that Paul had two little sisters, looked up at last and found that they were in a narrow street hung with paintings and sketches on each side. "What is this?"

"This is the rue de Tresor, where the artists sell their work."

"Certainly includes all kinds," Mollie murmured, looking from a dreamy landscape to a modern surrealistic painting. "What's this? A fractured staircase and a blue cat?"

"I think the cat is fractured, too," Paul said solemnly. Mollie giggled.

He peered over her shoulder at the canvas, and Mollie held her breath, feeling his closeness as he brushed her arm. Her stomach somersaulted again, and when he spoke, she had to focus all her attention just to catch his words.

"What?"

"Come this way; there is something you might like."

They ambled down the narrow street, crowded with tourists examining the pictures, stout women haggling over prices, and gray-haired gentlemen frowning wisely over the artistic techniques. Finally Paul found what he sought.

"Would you like your portrait done, mademoiselle?"

Mollie turned and saw the man with the sketch pad. She watched as he deftly sketched two children who stood still only under protest while their mother admonished them to stop wiggling and let the nice man finish their picture. A rough but recognizable chalk sketch was beginning to emerge on the blank sheet. The mother beamed, and the two children, released at last from their enforced inactivity, ran off down the street.

"John, Tammy, wait!" the woman shrieked as

she fumbled with her purse, trying to pay the man, collect her picture, and run after her impatient offspring all at once.

Mollie giggled, then discovered that Paul looked at her inquiringly. "Wouldn't you like a portrait?"

"Of me?" Mollie's eyes widened, then, impulsively, she spoke quickly before she lost her nerve. "Only if you will be in it, too."

"If you wish," Paul replied. He spoke to the artist in rapid French. The man picked up his chalk and motioned to them to stand closer together.

Paul moved obediently next to Mollie, and Mollie, breathing quickly, felt his shoulder brush her own. Then Paul reached out quite naturally and took her hand, holding it easily and firmly. Mollie, whose whole arm tingled from the contact, found that his grip was strong but careful; she needed no caution from the artist to stand absolutely still. She would have frozen the moment forever if she could. Instead she gazed at the artist, unable to suppress the smile that burst from inside her.

When the man finished, all too soon, they both moved forward to examine the finished work. Mollie saw that the girl on the paper wore a brilliant smile that only special excitement could explain, and her sparkling eyes lit up the page. But Mollie wasn't interested in her own likeness, though Paul examined it with rapt attention. She focused on Paul's picture, seeing new details that delighted her—the firmness of his chin, the wide, thoughtful forehead, the slight lift in one dark brow.

"*Merci beaucoup;* it's wonderful," she told the

man, who smiled in acknowledgment as Paul paid him.

"For you," Paul told her. Mollie took the sketch, careful not to crease it, and threw him a grateful glance.

"Thank you, Paul. I love it."

"But there is a price," the boy warned her.

Mollie, eyes wide, gazed up at him.

"You must give me one of your pictures, so I have something of you to keep."

Mollie blushed. "I will," she promised.

"Good."

Mollie rolled the sketch and tied it carefully with a ribbon from the next stall, and they strolled on through the streets.

When the came back to the Place d'Armes, Paul gestured to a waiting carriage.

"Would you like to ride in the *calèche*?"

"I'd love to," Mollie said, thinking that this would complete a perfect afternoon.

Paul spoke to the guide, who jumped down and unhitched the handsome chestnut, then started to help Mollie step up into the carriage, but Paul was there ahead of him.

Mollie, feeling like a grand lady, accepted Paul's hand and stepped into the carriage.

"I feel exactly like Cinderella," she breathed, as Paul took his place beside her. Shyly, he reached for her hand.

"You don't mind?"

"No," Mollie whispered.

Their guide snapped his driving reins, and the carriage moved forward at a sedate pace.

The driver gestured toward the imposing facade of the Chateau Frontenac, telling them how
the Comte de Frontenac, in 1690, was threatened
by an English fleet, who demanded the surrender
of his fortress.

" 'Tell your lord I will reply with the mouths of
my cannons,' Frontenac told him. And the enemy
fleet sailed away."

The gray-haired driver glanced back to see if
they appreciated the story and discovered that
Paul and Mollie were oblivious to his anecdote.
Deciding that his stories were wasted on these
passengers, the driver gave up and instead began
to hum softly, concentrating on guiding the horse
down the usual streets.

Mollie didn't even notice that the commentary
had ceased. "I'll always remember this," she told
Paul. "Thank you for a very special day."

"Moi aussi," he assured her quickly. "It is special to me, also, Mollie. I'm so glad you came to
Quebec."

"Me, too," Mollie agreed.

Paul squeezed her hand, then moved his left
arm and put it carefully around her shoulders.

Mollie, blissful with pure happiness, laid her
head back against his arm, and they watched the
colorful avenues of Quebec roll past them in contented silence.

Chapter 14

*T*he next week was filled with magic. Mollie and Paul tried their best to sample a little of everything at the festival and their days were crowded with music, laughter, and performers from around the world. It was a blissful period for Mollie. She couldn't remember ever having been happier. Secure in her bubble of joy, she forgot about time and place, and somehow felt sure that this would go on forever.

But then Cindy, one night at dinner, looked at the date on her watch and shook her head in disbelief. "Only one more week and we'll be home again. it's been a great trip, hasn't it?"

"Oui," Nicole agreed, although her eyes still held a shadow. "I've learned a lot, like how dumb I really am."

Cindy, her mouth full of delicious quiche, blinked,

and then decided she hadn't heard her sister correctly.

Mollie, still frozen with the reminder that their vacation was coming to an end, stared at Cindy in horror.

"I won't go home," she announced.

"Don't be ridiculous," Nicole snapped, thankful that Madame Gilbert had gone into the kitchen to take her dessert out of the oven.

"I won't; I'll get a job, rent a room—I won't go." Bursting into tears, Mollie jumped up and ran out of the room.

"What's wrong with her now?" Nicole asked wearily.

Cindy shook her head, but she looked thoughtful.

During the day, while she was with Paul, Mollie forgot the future, forgot everything except that Paul and she were together. On Monday they met early for a walk in the park, holding hands beneath the leafy canopies, talking about all the little things that they still didn't know about each other.

Paul told her about his dog. "His name is Goudron, like tar, you know, because he is so black. He's not very big; he stands about twenty centimeters. I have had him since I was six; he is quite old for a dog."

Mollie laughed. "Our dog is black, too, but he's huge. A boy once mistook him for a bear. He's a Newfoundland; his name is Winston. And we have two cats, Smokey and Cinders."

A sound of music made her pause, and Paul took her hand. "Come on; we will see the acrobats."

They joined the crowd around the street circus, and laughed at the antics of the clowns, and gasped as the acrobats leaped and tumbled.

Next there was a man on a unicycle, whose balance defied all possible laws of gravity. Then, after the audience applauded, Paul motioned Mollie on to watch a collection of life-sized marionettes. The puppets performed zany antics, and Mollie and Paul laughed along with the crowd of youngsters, then clapped when the wooden performers took their last bows.

They shared a delicious lunch of meat pie and buckwheat crepes with maple syrup at a small restaurant, while Paul told her about "sugaring-off."

"It depends on the weather," he told her, while Mollie licked a drop of syrup off her fingers. "In March or April, when it still freezes at night, but thaws during the day, the maple sap begins to run. Then everyone goes to the 'sugar shacks' in the maple groves. Lots of visitors come to sample the syrup and the thick maple taffy, or to take home maple sugar."

"It sounds like fun," Mollie said.

"It is. The children pour the syrup onto the snow to form hard candy in funny shapes. Everyone dances and sings the old songs, and the men drink 'caribou.' "

"What's that?" Mollie asked curiously.

"A mixture of alcohol and red wine—only for the strong of stomach!"

"Ugh!" Mollie grimaced at the thought, and they laughed together.

Then they went off to hear a concert by bag-pipe players and drummers. Mollie had to laugh at the sight of all these grown men marching along in their bright Scottish tartans. Next they heard an African drum quartet perform in color-ful native costumes. Mollie went home with the music still echoing in her ears and the memory of Paul's touch warming her heart.

One night they went to l'Agora and sat in the open air amphitheater with thousands of young fans, listening to Canadian and French rock sing-ers. During the day they saw theater and jazz groups and more clowns and story tellers. It was, as Paul had said, like one continuous party.

Even Nicole took some time off from her con-stant studying and dragged a reluctant Cindy off to see the Montreal Ballet. Cindy, who had been planning to accompany Roland and Antoine to see a troupe of acrobats, grumbled, but when the dance company began to perform, she quieted, impressed despite herself by the athletic control and strength displayed by the slender men and women on the stage.

"I bet he'd make a good hockey player," Cindy whispered as she watched the muscled principal dancer leap around the stage. "Look at the way he throws that girl all over the stage!"

"Shh," Nicole hissed at her sister.

But as the show continued, the beauty of the performance made Cindy forget all practical comparisons, and like Nicole, she spent the rest of the evening entranced by the dancers' lyrical grace.

"Now confess, you enjoyed it," Nicole said afterward.

Cindy nodded, a little surprised at herself. "It really was awesome," she agreed.

"Now about the symphony tomorrow—" Nicole went on.

Cindy groaned.

Mollie was oblivious even of her sisters. She spent her days and most of her evenings with Paul. Once she asked him about his abandoned hockey practice.

"It doesn't matter," he assured her. "We don't want to miss the festival, do we?"

"Mais, non," Mollie agreed, happy that he took so much pleasure in her company.

On Thursday Mollie and Paul saw two Inuit women from the far north stand almost face to face and perform "throat music," a deep guttural sing-song chant that astonished Mollie.

"It is an old Inuit tradition. Very unusual, yes?" Paul told her.

"I should say so," Mollie agreed.

Then the young pair searched for a free table in a crowded café. "Look," Mollie whispered, "that family is about to leave!"

"You grab the table," Paul told her, "I will summon the *garçon.*"

Mollie managed to slip into a chair before the middle-aged couple behind them could reach it.

Grinning triumphantly at Paul, she said, "Good teamwork!"

"The best!"

They sampled cream of leek soup and chicken croquettes, and later Mollie had to confess that she was too full even for dessert.

"Just as well," she said regretfully. "I'm probably going home with a couple of pounds of Quebec pastries on my waistline!"

'I think you are *la perfection,*" Paul insisted loyally. "Just right."

Mollie beamed at him, and they held hands under the table while they finished their sodas.

Then they watched stilt walkers from Belgium, in colorful seventeenth-century costumes, who engaged in an incredible jousting battle. Then a trio of musicians took the stage, and with dulcimer, flute, and fiddle, played haunting ballads.

"Mon père et ma mère . . ." they sang, and Paul translated softly for Mollie's benefit. "My father and my mother are from Locmine; they made a promise to marry me off." He gave her a mischievous glance, and Mollie's cheeks flushed. Paul held Mollie's hand tightly, and she found that the lump in her throat made it impossible to talk. She squeezed his hand, and they stood close together amid the crowd.

Then the next group of performers came out, couples dressed in cheerful, old-fashioned costumes. The girls wore dark red dresses covered with white aprons and trimmed with red and gold lace, with small white caps and white stockings. The young men were dressed in dark blue trousers, with blue jackets adorned with red and gold embroidery, and staid black hats embellished with red ribbon. The girls flipped open fans, and with coquettish expressions, began to dance.

"Look," Paul said, "it is a quadrille."

Mollie admired the graceful figures of the dance. "They make it look so easy."

"It's not hard; French folk dances are not complicated; you just have a good time."

Paul joined in the applause as the dancers completed their act. Then the music began again, and Mollie saw that some of the audience were joining the dancers on the platform.

"Come on," Paul urged, taking her by the hand. "This is a gavotte."

"Oh, I can't!" Mollie gasped, panicking at the thought of looking foolish in front of Paul.

"It's easy. Just follow me. We learned it in school when we were small," he assured her, and drew her firmly toward the platform.

They took their place with other smiling couples, and Mollie tried not to look totally bewildered.

"Like this," Paul said, showing her how to link little fingers. In this way, they formed part of a long chain of dancers, and the music, lilting and lively, began.

"Three steps forward," Paul directed, and Mollie hastened to follow his example.

"Then swing your right leg—so." Paul demonstrated, and Mollie, a step behind, hastened to catch up.

"Now back, step, then step forward."

Laughing, Mollie forgot her fear of looking silly

and followed as best she could. Paul smiled with her, and the other couples, laughing and dancing, didn't seem to mind that the California girl was not the most practiced of folk dancers.

"This is fun," she told him as they stepped forward again.

By the time the dance ended, Mollie was out of breath from laughing and kicking. But instead of moving back to the audience, Paul took her hand and kept her in place.

"Non, non," he told her. "We have just begun."

This time they clasped hands, and two couples stood in a single line, the women at an angle to the men. Now, Mollie discovered, each couple held only each other's hands; Paul's grip was warm and firm, and he smiled at her, his brown eyes sparkling.

Mollie glanced quickly at the other dancers and saw that the rest of the women had begun to dance in a slow circle around their partners.

Mollie, still clasping Paul's right hand, began to follow the pattern of the dance. Their eyes met as she circled and Mollie suddenly found it difficult to breathe. She was so close that she could see the delicate curl of his dark lashes where they fringed his eyes, and the way his upper lip lifted slightly as he smiled at her. Mollie felt the rest of the dancers, the music, all the world recede, while she and Paul turned in a charmed circle, conscious only of each other.

Paul gazed into her eyes as if he were entranced. Their steps slowed, regardless of the music's rapid tempo, and Mollie saw Paul move closer. She held her breath: he was so close, so close—and then he bent forward, and their lips touched.

One endless moment later, they realized that the music had stopped, and other couples were talking and laughing around them, heedless of the pair so lost in each other.

Paul and Mollie stepped away from the platform, threading their way through the people around the stage. Neither spoke until they had left the crowd behind them and reached the comparative privacy of a leafy glade of trees. Then Paul stopped in the shade of a large oak and pulled Mollie gently into his arms. This time their lips met firmly and sweetly, and the kiss lingered, while his arms encircled her in a strong, comforting embrace.

When they parted at last, Mollie had no words large enough to express what she felt. She hid her face briefly in the smooth cotton folds of his shirt, then felt him touch her cheek gently with his fingertips.

"All is well, *ma petite*?"

"Oh, yes," Mollied nodded, still breathless. "I've never been kissed before—not like that, Paul."

Paul nodded. "This is special. *Je t'adore*, Mollie."

"Me, too," Mollie whispered. She thought that her heart might burst from sheer joy, like a dam crumbling from the force of flood water behind it.

They kissed again, then held hands and walked through the park, talking furiously of fantastic future plans. Paul would complete his studies and become an engineer, and they would marry and

live in a cottage with red blossoms in the window-
boxes and a dog and cat to sit on the hearth.

It was a little like planning a doll's house, Mollie thought. Perhaps too much so. Paul, who had
picked a fragile white flower to tuck into her
blond hair, hesitated as he saw her frown, and the
light flower, caught by the slight summer breeze,
drifted away.

Mollie, watching it go, realized that all their
plans were really nothing more than dreams.

Paul seemed to catch her thought, because he
sighed and said, "Perhaps, after all, we are too
young to make such plans just yet, Mollie."

Mollie nodded sadly, even while she held tightly
to his other hand, dreading the thought that she
might have to let go of this first, wonderful passion.

"But this is our first love, yes?" His dark eyes
searched her blue ones, and Mollie nodded em-
phatically.

"Oh, yes, Paul."

"And the first love is special, they say. No other
is ever quite like it. We will always have that,
Mollie, and this summer to remember."

He pulled her into a impulsive embrace. Mollie
hid her face against his chest, and didn't know
whether to cry or to laugh.

They walked in the park till long past sunset, and
it was later than usual when Paul finally took her
home. They kissed briefly at the gate, then Mollie
hurried up the path, worried that Madame Gilbert
might have locked the big front door. She tried
the knob cautiously, and was relieved to find that
the door creaked open. Waving to Paul, she slipped

inside. But as she tiptoed in, Mollie found a silent figure sitting on the bottom stair.

"Cindy, what are you doing?"

"Waiting for you, shrimp."

Mollie, bracing herself for a lecture, looked defiant, but her sister only shrugged.

"Don't worry, I'm not going to tell you how selfish you're being; I'm too sleepy."

"I'm sorry I kept you up," Mollie began.

Cindy shook her head. "That's not what I mean. You know Paul hasn't been to hockey practice all week because he's too busy with you?"

"He said it didn't matter." Mollie's tone was defensive, but a small flicker of doubt shadowed her happiness.

"It does matter," Cindy contradicted. "A real athlete practices all year-round; that's what makes the difference between great and almost great, Mollie. And Paul is really a first-class player. I don't think you realize how good he is."

"Yes, I do," Mollie argued, angry that Cindy was trying to destroy her idyllic romance.

"Well, he won't be if he goes on spending all his time with you. And he needs a scholarship the other boys told me. You're not helping him, Mollie."

Cindy, too tired to argue, turned to go upstairs, unaware that Mollie had paused, stricken by the though that she might unknowingly harm Paul.

Then Cindy remembered what she had waited up to tell her sister. "Did you realize that tomorrow is Nicole's eighteenth birthday?"

"Oh, no," Mollie gasped. "I forgot all about it."

"Me, too," Cindy confessed. "Mom called to-

night while Nicole was still at the library studying
and you were out. She wanted to remind us about
Nicole's birthday.

Mollie bit her lip, feeling guilty.

Cindy added, "She'll call back tomorrow. But I
asked Madame Gilbert if we could make Nicole a
cake, if you think you can manage to come home
early tomorrow and help."

"I will," Mollie promised. "And I'll buy her a
present tomorrow."

"Good." Cindy yawned and started up the stairs.
But Mollie sat down on the step that Cindy had
abandoned and stared into the darkness, her mind
filled with thoughts of Paul. Was she really being
selfish? What was more important, being with
Paul, or making sure that his plans for a university education weren't threatened?

Mollie sighed. Unfortunately, the answer to her
question seemed obvious.

Chapter 15

*A*t the end of class on Friday, the instructor handed back their last assignment. Nicole, receiving her paper, murmured, *"Merci,"* but didn't have the nerve to open the cover and look at the grade. She waited till class was dismissed and everyone else had left the classroom before she stood up, gathered her books, and headed for the door.

About to step outside the classroom, Nicole glanced around, then unable to wait any longer, she lifted the front cover to see her grade.

She gasped. Another girl, just ahead in the hallway, turned back. "Nicole, are you all right?"

Nicole looked up to see Gabriella staring at her with concern. "It's my essay."

"Ah," the Canadian girl nodded in understanding. "The instructor, he is very strict."

"Yes, no—I mean, he wrote *'Bon travail!'*" Nicole looked bewildered. "'Good work'; I don't believe it."

"That is very commendable," the other girl said with a smile. "Why are you so surprised?"

"I thought he—he didn't like my work," Nicole confessed. "I've felt like such a dummy all through this course."

"Dummy?" The other girl looked puzzled.

"You know, stupid," Nicole explained.

Gabriella laughed. *"Mais non,* Nicole. You made some mistakes the first week, but this is very different for you, yes? You have done very well, I think."

"Merci," Nicole smiled back. "I was beginning to think that I would never survive college."

"Ah, you will do well, I am sure," the other girl told her generously. "You have been so—how do you say—apart from everyone, Nicole. I was afraid you were not happy."

"Today's my birthday," Nicole confessed impulsively. "And I guess I'm homesick."

"Permit me to treat you to a *café au lait,*" the other student offered.

Nicole smiled. It had hurt when neither of her sisters mentioned the special day at breakfast. They both had apparently forgotten. Now her spirits lifted for the first time all day.

"Merci beaucoup," she said brightly, and they walked off together.

When Nicole got off the bus and made her way

up the avenue toward the Gilbert residence, she thought she caught a glimpse of Cindy, but the tousled blond head disappeared inside the door, and Nicole, who thought for a moment her sister was waiting for her, shrugged and hugged her essay to her chest. At least she knew now that she wasn't a total failure!

Nicole entered the house quietly and was about to go up the stairs when a sudden chorus of shouts and whistles made her whirl around. Suddenly the dining-room doors were flung open.

"Happy birthday!" Cindy and Mollie shouted. Madame and Monsieur Gilbert stood behind them, smiling broadly. An elaborate *gâteau* sat in the center of the broad table, with several wrapped presents beside it; a large bouquet of red roses filled a crystal vase.

"Mom and Dad wired the flowers; aren't they gorgeous!" Cindy commented. "They'll be calling later; I wasn't sure what time you'd be home."

"We made the cake, with a lot of assistance from Madame Gilbert," Mollie said, glancing proudly at the elaborate confection. "Good thing she helped!"

Nicole felt a suspicious dampness blur her vision as she sank down into a dining-room chair. "I thought you'd forgotten."

Cindy, trying not to look guilty, said quickly, "Of course not—not your eighteenth birthday!"

"*Félicitations,* Nicole," Madame Gilbert said.

And her husband added, "We will open a bottle of champagne and toast your birthday before dinner, yes?"

He went into the kitchen, and his wife followed. Nicole dabbed at her eyes with a tissue.

"What's wrong, Nicole?" Cindy asked. She and Mollie stared at their big sister with concern.

"I was worried about Mollie, and *I'm* the one who's been homesick," Nicole confessed. "I thought I was a failure in my class; I really didn't think I was going to make it on my own."

The two younger Lewis sisters looked stunned. Then Mollie shook her head, patting her big sister on the shoulder.

"You expect too much of yourself, Nicole. You're going to be fine."

"I know that now," Nicole said, biting her lip to keep from smiling at the thought of Mollie reassuring *her*.

"And I know that I'll always have the love of my family, no matter how far away I am." She leaned close to sniff the delicate sweet scent of the roses.

"That's right," Mollie agreed. "Love doesn't depend on geography, not if it's real. Paul taught me that." She sighed a little, and Nicole looked at her more closely.

"This was more than another crush, wasn't it, Mollie?" Nicole realized. "You really are growing up."

The other two girls couldn't help grinning at Nicole's surprised discovery.

"But wasn't that why you didn't want to leave Quebec?" the eldest Lewis inquired.

Mollie nodded. "I know that wasn't very realistic or mature of me to think I should stay here forever. Besides, Paul was neglecting his hockey practice. He'll go back to work after I'm gone."

"That matters to you?" Cindy looked at her younger sister in obvious surprise.

"I didn't realize it would hurt him until you told me," Mollie said.

She looked away from her sisters' inquiring faces, struggling against the rush of sadness that threatened to overwhelm her whenever she thought of being separated from Paul. But Mollie refused to allow her sorrow to overwhelm the sweetness of the emotion she and Paul had shared.

Both girls stared at her. Then Nicole shook her head. "I don't know, Mollie. I'm not sure you're the same sister I brought to Quebec a few weeks ago!"

Mollie grinned. "Love does that to you," she told them wisely.

Cindy whistled. "Mollie's being sensible? What's the world coming to?"

"Madame Gilbert told me that we've been such delightful house guests, and so helpful around the house, that she'd love to have me, or any of us, come back next summer!" Mollie told them. "But let's hurry up now and get dinner on the table," she urged. "I invited Paul to come over later and have cake and champagne with us. You'll like him, Nicole."

"I'm sure I will," Nicole agreed, still slightly overwhelmed by the maturity her baby sister was displaying. *"Mon dieu,* I'm going to miss you two next fall."

For a moment she gathered them both into a big hug, and the three girls clung together.

"Whatever happens," Cindy reminded them, "no matter where we go, we'll always be sisters."

"Always!" the other two agreed.

Here's a sneak preview from HOLDING ON, the twelfth book in Fawcett's "Sorority Girls" series for GIRLS ONLY.

Ellie waited outside Roberts Music Hall. She shifted from foot to foot and wished for a breeze. It was hot standing in the sun, waiting for Jason to arrive for his graduation meeting. She'd convinced Laura to review Jason's agenda. The seniors were meeting in the theater for instructions, and then they would have their first practice outside.

From her position behind the opened door, she saw him approaching with the clarinet player from the band. She waited until he was close enough and then whispered, "Jason!"

He looked around and started to go inside when he didn't see anyone. She called again, and he peeked around the door. "Ellie! What are you doing here?"

"I need to talk to you." Her voice was husky and she swallowed, trying to clear it.

"But I've got a meeting in less than ten minutes."

"I know. It won't take long," she said quickly, before she lost all her nerve.

"Shouldn't you be in class?"

She nodded. "But this is more important."

That seemed to convince him. He came around the door and stood next to her, leaning against the brick building.

She gazed up into his beautiful eyes. Would she ever see them look at her again the way she had drawn them in her sketch? After this talk, things might never be the same for them. She was afraid, but she knew she had to do it. "Jason. I have to know how you feel about me."

His jaw tightened, but the emotion and fear in Ellie's eyes must have told him she was deadly serious. He took a minute to think. "A year ago I would have laughed at anyone who told me I'd be dating a Pearl."

"Please don't tell me I'm not your type," Ellie interrupted, in spite of her promise to give him a chance to say whatever he needed to say. "I know that's not true."

"You're right." He put a hand on her shoulder. "That's not true, and I don't want to lie to you. I care about you too much to do that, Ellie."

Hope started to flutter in her heart, but it settled quickly. The sadness in his eyes told her she wouldn't like everything he was going to say. But she believed he was finally going to be honest with her. Wasn't that what she wanted?

"I was afraid to fall in love with you," he said softly. "I thought if you didn't want a guy like Sam Taylor, a basketball star, then you couldn't want me. I felt a little bit sorry for Sam. Even before we got together, I could imagine how hard it would be for a guy to lose you."

"You're not losing me," she whispered, her hand itching to touch his face and smooth away the worry;

but she didn't dare. She read his deep blue eyes and her heart ached for him. They told her he treasured their memories as much as she did, and that the past few weeks had been painful for him, too.

"Ellie." He shook his head slowly. "You are the most special girl I've ever met. I loved you ... I still love you." He closed his eyes. "But you want promises that I can't make. I don't know what will happen in our future. Things are changing in both our lives, and it's very possible our paths are moving in different directions."

She looked away, desperately trying to blink back her tears. Biting her lip helped some, but it did nothing for the lump in her throat.

He lifted his hand off her shoulder and gently touched her hair. "Are you all right?"

She sniffed and tried her voice. "I'm okay. I even think I understand."

He caught her chin with his hand and turned her face toward him. She knew he could see the tears in her eyes. Although things looked hazy, she saw him blinking, too.

"Ellie, I don't want to hurt you. We'll be together whenever we can this summer, but I can't predict what will happen in the fall." He leaned down and kissed her gently on the forehead. "Will you come to the graduation party my parents are having for me next Friday night?"

Ellie swallowed twice. She didn't want to read too much into his invitation, because she just couldn't stand much more disappointment. Cautiously, she said, "I'd like to come."

He tried to smile. "Good. I thought we could go somewhere afterward for our own celebration."

"That would be great." Her voice was husky with

emotion. After all that had happened in the past few weeks, he still wanted her to be with him at this special time.

Jason cleared his throat. "Ellie?" When she looked up at him, he reached out to softly touch her hair. "I can't see into the future, but I can promise you one thing—you will always be with me where it counts." His lips brushed hers lightly. "In my heart."

Her first tear rolled down her cheek, and she closed her eyes to avoid facing any more reality for the moment. She felt him moving away, and she knew the second he was gone.